Marionette

A Zombie Series

SB Poe

ISBN: 9781980290742

Marionette

For my family

CONTENTS

The Day the World Ends

Starts Just Like Every Other Day

***

When the Black Death hit it decimated nearly a fourth of all mankind. They were sure it was the end of times. They were wrong, but while it was happening, when people were dying all around and cries for help went unanswered, they had only one word for it: Apocalypse.

***

"AP Report: The outbreak of rabies in Madagascar has spread to Africa. This current outbreak was recognized by the World Health Organization just 48 hours ago. The rapid spread of this outbreak has prompted US State Department officials to impose a strict NO/FLY policy for US citizens intending on traveling to or from Africa, Australia, and Madagascar. The State Department letter says this restriction is temporary and that airlines will hopefully work with customers to reschedule flights. We advise US Citizens within affected areas to reach out to their nearest consulate with questions."

Whispers

The weather was starting out just fine. A cold snap was rolling through at midday and the winds were picking up. The temps were already falling and JW Toles was looking forward to the afternoon. He was headed to his little 180/acre piece of Alabama timberland. Complete isolation. JW likes to have that at times. Kate, his wife, knows that, and it's why she encouraged him to buy the land in the middle of nowhere. The boys enjoy it during hunting season but this wasn't hunting season, so he would be alone. JW had spent about ten years in the Army on the shiny part of the spear before he had to quit. Kate knew why he needed to be alone sometimes. She knew he was a really good man with some terrible demons. He never drank, rarely yelled, never hit, never abused, but he was hard. He was not diplomatic. It made for awkward social interactions, so he didn't interact socially. Kate made excuses early in their marriage but as time wore on she would just say, "JW doesn't get out much" and leave it at that.

For his part, JW knew it made things hard for Kate, and that is why he agreed to go to the VA. He found a good doc who helped. He was a mostly normal dad at his kids' soccer games when they were younger and as they went into high school, he went to their football games and baseball games. Most dads went to practice too, but JW didn't enjoy standing around and talking. Well, mainly talking.   But today wasn't about any of that, today was about being alone and JW was excited. It was fall break and Kate, being a teacher, was out of school. Josh and Scott, being a junior and freshman respectively, were out too. Josh was leaving tomorrow to head to a friends house on the lake for a few days and Scott and Kate were going to spend the week pulling out all the Christmas boxes including the lights that JW would be stringing up around the house in a few weeks. Everyone had their plans.

After an early lunch, Josh filled his backpack with Vienna sausage cans and long john underwear. He had his sleeping bag and fishing gear. Kate was mainly looking forward to having the house mostly empty. Kate enjoyed reading in the quiet, which was rare with a house full of boys (JW included, she would joke).

"Hey Dad," Scott called from his room, "Can you come in here for a sec?"

JW walked into Scott's room. He was leaned back in an ergonomic computer chair in front of what looked to JW like some kind of multiscreen CIA spying display. Scott's workstation was slightly impressive. Scott was a gamer. He enjoyed coding and met some game creators online, helping beta test games for them. He didn't make much money doing it, but they paid for all his gear and his Internet bill. Kate didn't really love it, but JW convinced her that if Scott could make a living playing video games, more power to him.

"Have you been watching this stuff out of Madagascar and the rabies thing?" Scott asked. "Not really, just heard some stuff on the news. Sounds bad, but they have dealt with this kind of stuff there for a while with plague outbreaks."

"Not this kind, Dad. Look,"

Scott pulled up a YouTube video and hit play. A cellphone video started playing. There was a crowd of people walking down the street. Not marching, or chanting or holding signs, but just walking all together. The video is shot over the shoulders of soldiers or policemen; they are pointing rifles at the crowd. They open fire and the first lines of people go down. They fire again and most of the rest hit the ground.

"Watch this" Scott says.

They all start to get up. Each one stands and starts shuffling towards the camera again. The police fire again. This is repeated at least two more times before the cameraman and the police break off running.

Scott opened another video; this one is of a man standing on a dirt street in Africa. He is walking in the same aimless gait as the crowd in the other video. It looks like some kind of aid camp because you can see a white tent with a red cross on the hill. The person filming is speaking English.

"This man died less than one hour ago. I saw him die. He came back and attacked a nurse. This is real. We need help." The video ends.

"If you have to say it's real, it probably isn't." JW smirked.

"No Dad, I think this may be bad."

"It's bad, Scott, but this isn't real. You know that. Rabies doesn't do this. I am sure there are some incidents of attacks but that (pointing at the monitor) isn't what rabies does. Ok?"
"Not really," Scott says as he turns back towards the large screen in the middle.

JW walked back into the living room with

a little smile on his face.

"What is that look for?" asked Kate

"Oh nothing, Scott just thinks zombies are on the loose."

"Is that all?" Kate smiled.

Scott was incredibly smart. He thought about things in ways that made JW and Kate wonder if he made more sense than they were capable of understanding. JW said he thought logistically. He planned ahead. That was what made him a good game tester. He knew if getting from point A to point B made sense in the game and if it was worth the effort. But zombies? Kate smiled again.

JW went out to his truck to make sure everything was ready to go. He had packed for a few days of camping. He always carried his pistol and on this trip he was carrying his little civilian version M4 style rifle so he could maybe shoot some wild hogs. They had recently been seen in the area and JW had read an article about how this rifle was almost perfect for pig hunting because it just was. So JW, not really needing an excuse but wanting to have one, used that as the justification to buy one. He loved it. It felt familiar. Anyway, he was looking forward to the week ahead.

Kate had picked out three books to read and Josh was completely ready to get going, although he would have to wait till tomorrow because his buddy had to work today. He was going to spend the day relining his fishing reels. Kate also planned to take advantage of Josh and have him help bring everything down, so after he leaves she can just kick back and relax.

JW came through the kitchen door just as Kate was informing Josh of his coming servitude. Josh didn't seem surprised.

"Well, guess I'll be heading out," JW said.
"Well, guess you need to give us a hug," Kate replied. He did.

JW went out to his truck and turned the key. He pulled out of the driveway and looked back through the rearview mirror. He caught Kate, Josh and Scott all standing in the big bay window of the kitchen, waving at him.

"Wish I could take a picture, JW thought as his eyes returned towards the street in front of him.

In 76 miles, over one river and one lake and around a bunch of bends in the road and one 2.5 miles drive down an old dirt road he would be alone. He turned on the radio to his favorite station. It was talk radio and news. No music. Music put him in moods. Sometimes good moods, sometimes bad, so no music.

All the way there he listened to the news. Between coverage of the latest political crises, there was Madagascar. The virus had hit epidemic levels, and the government was having difficulty responding. The UN and WHO had declared an emergency, and the US was teaming with Britain to send a couple thousand troops to help with security. JW couldn't help but keep thinking about Scott's videos. He smiled as he turned down the dirt road. He stopped. He always stopped at this spot. The creek he stopped over marked the southern boundary of his property and he had spent a tiny fortune putting this bridge and road in. The gate was just across the bridge. JW liked to stop on the bridge. He looked at the creek running below and smiled. He moved on. He pulled up to the gate. He got out, unlocked it, and drove the truck through. He got out again and locked it behind him.

***

"The disease that has been ravaging Madagascar and Africa has spread to Europe and there are possible reports of cases on the West Coast, more to follow."

***

The radio played as he drove towards the wide spot that served as his campground.

Another 1/4 mile. His phone rang.

"Hey honey," It was Kate. "Just wanted to let you know we got all the lights down and they went straight into the trash. Only one strand lit up and we couldn't trace anything out."

"Ok, kind of random reason to call, but Ok," JW said

"Well, also, I have been watching TV and talking to Scott." "
"Oh, this is gonna be good." "

"Stop it, John, I am more than a little nervous and now they say it has reached the US."

"Yeah, I just heard that, too. What do you want me to do?"

"I want you to stop your truck before you get too far out for cell service and start calling anyone you know from your army days and find out what the hell is going on. I want you to do that right now, and I want you to have an answer to me as quickly as you can. And I want you to consider coming home." Kate's voice rising through the phone.

"Slow down, let me stop and" a deer crossed the road and JW slammed on the brakes, phone flying out of his hand and straight against the windshield.

"Shit." He reached for the phone. "Hey, you still there? "

"Yes, what the hell just happened?"

"A damn deer run across the road. I'm fine. Did you say you wanted me to come home?"

"Yes."

"Are you serious?"

"Yes."

"Let me call you back. I will stop and call a guy or two who may know something and call you back."

"Ok, hurry" Kate said

"Love you bye" and JW hung up the phone. He opened his contacts and found Bridger Preston. Bridger had eaten the same dirt as JW in the Army and had parlayed that into a part-time analyst role on a major news network. He and JW had been tight,' but not in a while. They still exchanged phone numbers and Christmas cards. He called the number.

" Hey, JW, is that you?"

"Yeah, it's me Bridge. How you doing?"

"Ok, under the circumstances."

"What does that mean Bridger?"

"Well, first of all, my damn spot today got pushed to 5 am tomorrow, because of the damn news reports of this virus thing hitting the West Coast. It's fake news, and the government is about to make a formal statement on that and they are also going to tell folks that this is completely overblown."
"And is it?" JW asked

"I don't know. Right now, I am buying a couple

of cans of beans to ride it out." Bridger said half jokingly.

"But the virus, I have seen some videos."

"Yeah, I saw em too. Don't know what to make of them. I mean come on. That looks like a zombie movie."

"That's what my youngest said just a few hours ago."

"Well, I can't argue with him. The only question is, was it real?"

"Was it?" JW asked.

"JW, are you asking me if there are zombies in Madagascar?"

He could hear the smirk on the other end of the phone.

"Alright, I get ya. Be safe and thanks."

"Don't get bit." JW could hear Bridger's laugh even after he hung up the phone.

JW sat there processing what he had just been told. His buddy was as skeptical as he was, but it was becoming more and more apparent that this virus might become a problem. Ok, that is not unreasonable. The next step, reanimated corpses, was unreasonable. And reason wins.

"Hey honey, I just got off the phone with Bridger Preston."

"And?"

"Well, he says the virus has not spread to the US, and the government is about to say that and that the government will also say that everything is under control."

"We're screwed."

"KATE, I'm shocked."

"Yeah right, anyway, what did Bridger say?"

"He said it's a virus, they spread, we find a cure or something, life goes on. I know you said you wanted me to come home, and I will, but I am going to stay up here tonight. I won't make camp. I'll just build a fire and sleep in the bed of the truck."

"What about Josh leaving tomorrow?" she asked

"Let me sleep on it. I'll keep my phone charged with the truck and keep tabs on the news, but you can try to have him stay home."

"What do you mean try? I will just tell him," Kate sounded exasperated.

"He's seventeen and even if you tell him you can't physically make him. Catching flies requires honey."

"Who the hell would want to catch a fly?" Kate said

They said their goodnights and JW assured Kate he would be home before noon. He parked and plugged his phone into the truck. He kept the key in the radio position to give juice to his phone and he turned up the volume to hear the news. He got out in the wide spot of the road and started to build a campfire. He had brought along several larger logs that he had chopped and stacked for these occasions last spring. He had enough for the week. He needed all the little stuff to get the fire going and the woods can provide plenty. He had gathered an armful and was turning to head back when he lost his footing. He had managed to step right into a small rodent hole that he hadn't seen and it was just enough that when he turned his weight shifted the wrong way and he fell. He was laughing at himself on the way down, right until the moment his head made contact with the rock he also hadn't seen.

***

"Reports of the virus outbreak in the US were in error. US government spokesman says the virus is being monitored. The spokesman also says the US government is confident in its abilities to combat this through educational efforts and expects the public to understand the mild threat and to take appropriate precautions should that become necessary."

***

The news played through the entire night across the wide spot on the road. JW slept.

When JW finally woke, it was quiet. And dark. He glanced up at the shooting stars that crossed the sky above him. He looked at his watch. 4:15. He assumed it was morning. Damn, his head hurt. And he was cold. And dressed.

"What the hell happened?" he thought.

Then he started to remember. He remembered tripping. He remembered gathering wood. It was like his memory was coming back in pieces. Then he remembered his conversation with Kate. Kate, oh shit. He thought.

He stumbled towards the truck and reached up to touch what was causing his head to hurt and he saw the blood on his hand. Not much, but definitely blood. He wondered if he had a concussion. He didn't feel sick, but he was a little wobbly. When he got to the truck, he opened the door expecting to hear the bong bong bong of the door chime but instead only silence. He saw his phone with the charger cable attached and realized the radio was no longer playing.

"Great." he thought, knowing a dead battery meant he would have to get someone to come rescue him.

He hated that. He picked up the phone to call his family and realized it was still 4:30 in the morning. He could wait. Instead, he opened up his newsfeed and started reading about Madagascar.

Morning

Kate lay awake. She had drifted off for a little while, nervously. Now she was awake again, and the clock said 4:20, so she knew she hadn't slept much. She turned the TV back on and saw the test bars. She panicked a little and realized it was local and flipped the channel to national news. Madagascar.

**

"AP sources are reporting widespread power outages throughout Australia and Eastern Africa. The UAE and Saudi Arabia are reporting cases of the rabies virus, now being dubbed the Marionette virus. Reports of multiple attacks by mobs of infected wreaking havoc throughout some parts of Madagascar have yet to be confirmed. US officials are monitoring the situation and as of now there are still no confirmed reports of the Marionette virus in the US despite earlier reports from West Coast news sources. Those sources have not been able to confirm any treatment at any hospitals. We will continue to monitor the situation. In other news,

President Wilson canceled a planned trip to Texas and instead will fly to Camp David to start a long holiday weekend."

***

Kate relaxed a little. After listening to Scott last night and watching his "news" videos, she had expected to awaken to the trumpets sounding and some kind of dragon thing crawling out of the ocean with a tattoo of some numbers on its head or hand. The details on that part had escaped her, apparently. But presidents don't go on long weekend trips if the end times are upon us. Or do they? She was pretty sure they didn't, so she felt a bit more relaxed. She climbed out of bed and made her way into the bathroom to do her morning business. She walked into the kitchen and flipped on her single serve coffee maker. It always took it a minute to warm up, so she picked up her phone to check her e-mail. 47 new messages. As she was performing the ritual of cleaning out her inbox, one of the subjects caught her eye. "Family

Preparedness Plan" She opened it up. It was some kind of survival/canning device, as best she could tell. It looked like a camo pressure cooker, and Kate giggled a little. She was pretty sure that if things got so bad that you needed to camouflage your kitchen ware, there wasn't any coming back.

"Mom, mom, come in here quick" Scott called from his room, surprising Kate that he was up this early.

She went to Scott's room, and he had a feed from the BBC on his main screen. The scroll said *"Marionette arrives in Spain"* and the images were unbelievable. It was a feed from a traffic camera and it wasn't showing traffic. It was showing hundreds of people just ambling around in the middle of an intersection that should be filled with cars and buses. The cars and buses were there, but the cars had their doors open and the buses were empty. Every person in the images was ambling the same way she had in at least a dozen other feeds Scott had shown her throughout the previous evening.

"Scott, this can't be real. It just can't be."

"Mom, I am connected to the whole gaming world. These folks tend to not spend too much time giving out personal information because they don't want to get doxxed if they pissed the wrong guy off. I am seeing folks putting pictures, phone numbers and addresses all over the place begging for help. And then they just go dark. This is bad."

"Ok, I'll call your father. Go wake up Josh."

"Josh left about an hour ago."

"What?"

"Yeah, he said he was gonna get a head start and just meet Bill there."

"Shit."

Her phone lit up in her hand.

Her 5:00 a.m. alarm.

"Shit shit double shit." Kate said out loud, thinking it wasn't, as she turned off her alarm.

She called Josh.

"Josh, where are you?" Kate asked.

"I just pulled up to the lake house, and I am gonna sit here and wait for Bill."

"No, you are going to come home right now."

"Excuse me?"

"Josh, I want you home right now. This Marie Antoinette virus has me very worried and..."

"Wait, wait, wait, the Marie Antoinette virus? Do you mean the Marionette virus?"

"I don't give a damn what it's called. I want you to come home."

"Mom, I just got here."

"Now, home."

"Yes, mama" Josh surrendered on the phone.

But he figured he was at the lake. He had snuck a six-pack of beer and dammit he was going to walk down to the water and drink a beer. Five A.M. is still five o'clock. Mom would just have to wait a few minutes more.

Kate called JW.

"Good morning honey, what time you heading home?" Kate asked. Surprised at how quickly JW answered the phone.

"About that." JW responded a bit sheepishly.

"About what?" Kate asked. Relieved to hear his voice as though she just needed to make some kind of connection with him, which reminded her again of just how nervous she was.

"Well, genius here managed to fall asleep and let the truck battery run down. It's no big deal. I will just walk back out to the main road and flag someone down to give me a jump." JW was making it up as he went now, but he was hoping she didn't notice. She noticed.

"Really, John, you are going to flag someone down and say, Hey my truck is broke down back here in these woods and I need you to let me get in your car and ride with you back into these woods off the road where nobody can see you so you can help with my truck. Really? That doesn't sound axe murdery at all. Now tell me what happened and what we need to do."

"The battery is dead. That's it. I left the key on, but I don't want you to come get me. Just send Josh."

"Josh isn't here. He went to the lake, but I called him and he should be on his way home now."

"Well, call him back and tell him to come get me. He's halfway here already if he is at Bill McFarland's place."

"Why can't you call him?"

"I think I may need to start conserving my phone battery."

Kate hung up the phone with Josh,

slightly angry that he had not already left the lake but glad he was still up that way so he could go get JW.

She turned to the big bay window and looked out into the front yard. The Alabama sky was that gray October color that usually meant football championships and pumpkin patches.

"Please, bring my boys home." Kate said to no one in particular.

Bridger Preston walked into the local affiliate in Nashville at 4:30 for his satellite spot about the latest arms deal between Israel and the UK, which really wasn't that big of a deal, but someone decided to give it 3 minutes. He was still amazed that he worked in a news business that prided itself on being 24 hr. news but never seemed to manage to give any story more than 3 minutes. If you have 24hrs, you should be able to devote some time to serious discussion and not just sound bite journalism. But what the hell did he know? He was just an analyst, paid to analyze things. He didn't want to steer too far out of his lane.

As he entered the control room, the first thing he noticed was the quiet. Admittedly it was 5 in the morning, but usually there were still folks shuffling around and talking. This morning everybody was just watching the feeds coming on the banks of televisions in the back. BBC, CNN, FOX, Al Jazeera and his network all carrying, in one form or another, stories about the Marionette virus. A scene from a street camera in Spain, a dusty road somewhere in East Africa and other odd scenes, streamed across the back wall. The one that caught Bridger's attention was the same one that had drawn the control room from their duties. In larger than normal type across the bottom of feed from Spain.

"FIRST CASE OF MARIONETTE VIRUS CONFIRMED IN NYC.

WHITE HOUSE TO MAKE STATEMENT

SOON."

Bridger read it again. And again. His mind was working through all the ramifications. He had spent his life trying to explain to people what the outcomes of any particular decision could mean in the long run. By working through the ramifications, you could reasonably predict different scenarios playing out. If you could see all the outcomes that put you ahead of the game, if you can see all the outcomes, reduce it down to one and be right? Well, that's why they pay Bridger Preston the big bucks.

Bridger thought about the strange conversation from the previous evening. JW Toles. Damn, he hadn't talked to JW in a year or two and except for getting a Christmas card last week he hadn't thought about him in a few months. He was thinking about him now. JW had been a good soldier and Bridger respected him. When he first got to JW's unit, JW had only been there about six months, which made him the next newest guy. Bridger's arrival got the

FNG label off of JW and for that reason alone
JW was always kind of grateful for Bridger's
arrival: their friendship came later.

Bridger kept playing it through his head.
If JW Toles had come out from his little world to
contact him, there was something to be
concerned about. JW was not the kind of guy to
just pick up the phone and call for a chat about
some virus in Madagascar. He was beginning to
wonder how JW always seemed to have his
"spidey-senses" tuned to just the right thing.
When they were in the big ashtray, JW had
always seemed to sense which buildings to pay
more attention to than others. It seemed
Madagascar had been the right "building".

He decided he needed more
information, so for now he was just like
everybody else who was waking up on the east
coast of the US, watching the TV and wondering
what the hell was happening?

JW decided to walk back to the gate so he could meet Josh. He figured by the time he walked the half-mile back he wouldn't have to wait very long. He grabbed his backpack without thinking and slung it over his shoulders. As soon as it was on his back, he realized he would be coming right back when Josh got here but something told him just to carry it with him, it would be good exercise. He shut the door of the truck and started walking. He got about ten feet from the truck and turned back to grab his rifle. He just couldn't bring himself to leave it unattended in his truck, even in the middle of nowhere. It was a habit. Loaded down with his backpack and rifle carried in his right hand, JW had a brief moment and laughed. He did his best to ignore the fact that the thing that screwed with his head the most was how much he missed doing the shit that screwed his head up.

He started down the road. He was wearing a pair of GI issue pants that he had bought on his last visit to the VA Commissary, with a pair of longjohns underneath. He had on two long sleeve t-shirts and a fleece camo top with a frogtog jacket. All of his clothes had that slept in feel and nothing really felt like it was on right. He stopped. He dropped his pack and laid his rifle across it. He unbuttoned his pants and re-tucked his shirts in, so nothing was all bunched up. He got everything buttoned back up and slung his pack back on. As he turned, he thought he saw someone walk across the road around the next corner. He did a double take but didn't see anything.

"Probably just another deer." He thought, as he unconsciously chambered a round into the rifle.

He started down the road again. A little more comfortable and a lot more alert. He walked to the point where he thought he had seen something (someone?) and stopped. He didn't see any sign of anything and no obvious tracks in the road. He looked at the honeysuckle growing just off the road and decided it had just been a deer standing here feeding. He had about another quarter mile to go and decided to stop and call Josh.

He pulled up Josh in his contacts and hit send. No service. It was spotty all along this road. He kept walking.

Josh was about three miles from the turn off to the bridge road. He called it the bridge road. His dad and brother called it the creek road. But they were wrong. He was rounding a bend when he saw the truck on the side of the road. He slowed down. As he passed, he noticed the passenger door was open, but nobody was in the truck and nobody was standing by the truck. As a matter of fact, he didn't see anybody, anywhere. Both sides of the road give way to fields that run to the woods 100 yards away, so he could see a pretty good area. No one. Odd.

He rounded the bend and started down the last stretch of paved road. His turn was about 2 miles down. Even though he would probably get fussed at for using his phone while driving, he called his dad.

JW could see the gate and was halfway hoping to see Josh waiting. He knew it shouldn't be too long. His pocket vibrated.

"Dad, I'll be there in about five minutes," Josh said.

"Can I assume you pulled over and put the vehicle in park to make this phone call?" JW said in his most "sound like a father." voice.

"Nope, bye" Josh said, and the line went dead.

JW smiled. He and Josh had a strange relationship. They both grew into who they were together. JW was trying to piece a life together from a bunch of fragments when Josh came along. They bonded over things that had been therapy for JW, fishing, hunting and just being outdoors. They had been as much comrades as father and son when Josh was young and they had fun. As Josh got older, JW kind of withdrew from him. Josh had rebelled a little in middle school as kids in middle school do and JW wasn't quite sure how to handle it, so he didn't. He watched Kate step up and help guide Josh through those years. Ever since then, there had been this strange space between them. They still had fun and laughed, but it had changed. JW couldn't quite figure it out.   As he was thinking about this, he saw Josh coming down the road to the creek. He walked up to the gate and unlocked it. Just as he did, two very low, very fast and very loud military aircraft raced over his head. JW instinctively ducked to his knees and looked up. Josh heard the roar and slammed on the brakes because that's what teenagers do when they panic. The rear of the SUV decided this was the perfect moment to see what was going on up front.

JW watched as Josh lost control and spun completely around in the middle of the road, looking straight back where had he just traveled. He stopped, put the SUV in park, and opened the door.

"Well, that was fun." he said, seeing his father hustling across the bridge towards him.

"You, ok?"

"Yeah, just a little shaky. What happened to you?" Josh said, making a motion towards his own forehead.

JW reached up, mirroring Josh's motion, and touched the spot on his head that hurt. He had almost forgotten about it.

"Oh, I just bumped it gathering wood. No biggie." JW said.

"Well, ok, let's get the truck," Josh said, starting to get back in his SUV

"I think I am just gonna leave it here. We can come back and get it in a day or two. You can just bring me up here when you come back up to the lake and we can get it then." JW said without really knowing why.
"I locked the gate already. Let's go home."

Josh, not even trying to figure out his Dad's logic anymore, just shut the door and started the engine. JW loaded his pack and rifle into the back seat and climbed into the passenger side.

"Maybe we can grab a bite on the way home," JW said, and they started back down the dirt road again.

Kate stood staring at the pantry. It was pretty well stocked. Her and JW had struggled when they first got married. They would scrape together 75 cents to go buy a roll of toilet paper when things got really tight. They had worked hard through JW's problems but it was a full time effort. JW had held several jobs since they got married but he never held any job more than a few years. Most jobs no more than a few months, and one famously for about an hour and a half. It created a lot of uncertainty about the future when you're buying toilet paper by the roll. JW finally got some help from the VA and had settled into a good job checking gas lines for the state. He spent most of the time monitoring data from his computer but occasionally he would have to go and ride the gas lines to check them. He enjoyed that part enough. It didn't pay great, but he got a check from the VA too and with Kate's income things had stabilized. After being that broke, their combined income now felt like winning the lottery. They had enough money to pay all the bills on the first of the month. They could keep the pantry stocked and go out to eat occasionally. That was the wish list they made twenty-five years ago when they used to lay in their bed and listen to the couple in the apartment above them beat their head against the headboard.

As she looked in the pantry, she made a meal plan in her head. She decided to make chili for supper. She had the beans and the tomatoes and knew she had the sausage and beef in the freezer. She had crackers but not oyster crackers.

JW really liked oyster crackers and Kate wished she had some to make up for being a nervous Nellie asking him to come home. She needed oyster crackers.

"Scott, come with me to the store, I need to get something."

"What do you need?" Scott called from his room

"I *need* you to come out here and go with me to the store, now."

Scott reluctantly emerged from his room.

"Can I drive?"

"Grab the keys." Kate said.

She didn't know if letting Scott drive was a great idea, but she was trying to hide her underlying nervousness and letting him drive would be completely normal since he was about a month away from graduating from a learner's permit to his drivers license.

They pulled out of the garage in Kate's

big SUV. All her friends had these mid-sized SUV's that can't decide if they are an all-purpose vehicle or a station wagon. Kate liked the height of her full size SUV, she felt like she could see everything. Actually it was a real pain in the ass to see anything that wasn't right in front of you but Kate had all the lane warning and parking features you could pack onto it. Kate will be the first on the block to buy a self-driving full size SUV. She tells JW that it would be like having an on demand chauffeur that drives you wherever you want to go whenever you want to get there. Think about it, you could get in your big old SUV tell Jeeves to head to Dallas, go to sleep in the back and wake up in Dallas. How freaking cool would that be? JW says it would take Jeeves about two weeks to figure out that he doesn't need these useless, fleshy bags of water around and it would be sayonara. JW doesn't get it.

The grocery store was only about a two miles from their house, as the crow flies, but it took about ten minutes to get there navigating through their neighborhood. The neighborhood had one entrance. It wasn't gated, but it had a security camera that monitored who came in and out so if something happened they had a good chance of finding a vehicle that was out of place. The Toles lived on a cul-de-sac at the back of the neighborhood. Their backyard was against an area of woods that ran almost five miles deep before it reached railroad tracks and just beyond, the river. Construction of the neighborhood had stopped during the last recession. The original plans supposedly had the neighborhood extending deeper, but they ran out of money. JW and Kate had bought the last house in the neighborhood for a steal. Truly. They paid a fourth of what the market value was prior to the crash. They were lucky. They had been getting their finances straight just before the crash and since they didn't own anything, the crash was more of a news event for them. Kate was a teacher and JW was 'flexible'. JW used his VA loan, and they bought themselves a house. Kate made it a home.

As they reached the neighborhood entrance, they noticed a sheriff's deputy parked beside the road. It wasn't unusual to see them there because they would watch for people running the stop sign at the four-way stop at the entrance. The crossroad had once been the main road between north of the river and south of the river about fifty years ago. The town had grown, and the route was moved east with a highway that crossed the river on the big beautiful six-lane bridge. The route at Kate's neighborhood was now mostly local traffic. If you go straight you end up at the new highway. Turn left and you head down to the river and the old bridge and beautiful little elementary school where Kate teaches fourth grade. Turn right and go about a mile and on your left is Magix. Known around the Toles house as simply *the store*. They turned right.

As they turned into the parking lot Kate was surprised that it wasn't full. She had been so nervous earlier she had half expected it to a shopping frenzy. They parked and went inside.

She guided the cart straight to aisle 7. That was where they kept the bread. She got halfway down the aisle before she realized that while they kept bread on aisle 7, they did not keep oyster crackers on aisle 7. She walked back down the aisle and scanned the overhead signs for crackers. Aisle 4. Away she went. She found oyster crackers and threw two bags into her cart.

"Really? That's what we came for? Oyster crackers." Scott asked.

"Your father likes them with chili. So yes." Kate stated.

She walked down the aisle absently adding cans that were on sale to her cart. "Does dad really like this stuff too?" Scott asked sarcastically.

"No, I just wanted to pick up a few things while we are here." Kate said.

Her mind was ticking off a list of things

that Kate felt like she really needed, for some reason. She went to the water aisle and grabbed two cases, ignoring her powerful urge to grab more. She grabbed some rice and dry beans. She had grabbed a decent stock of canned goods but she wanted to add to it. As she turned down the aisle, she saw an older woman. Their eyes met and Kate realized that the woman had the same sort of list running through her head. Kate stopped and looked around.

"We need to leave now." Kate whispered to Scott.

"Yeah, there is a weird vibe in here." Scott agreed.

They went to the registers and starting checking out. Kate looked at the young man checking her out and smiled. He smiled back. She could see it in his eyes too. Everybody is wondering if they should just panic and hoping someone doesn't step over the edge first. Kate and Scott pushed their cart, now all bagged up, out to their SUV. As they pulled away, Kate noticed the parking lot had filled up.

As they turned back into their neighborhood, she noticed the deputy was gone. They drove home. They walked into the kitchen and unloaded their stuff. Kate started getting things together for making the chili and reached over and flipped on the TV so she could hear the news.

JW reached down and started changing the radio in Josh's SUV.

"What are you doing, I like that song." Josh said.

"Just gonna try to catch a bit of news." JW said landing on the station he wanted.

***

"The White House briefing is expected to begin in just a few minutes. We expect them to address the confirmed case of Marionette virus in New York and also address the level of concern coming out of other parts of the world as this strange infection spreads. There are reports of almost unbelievable atrocities coming out of Africa and Australia. Mr. Martin, the White House Spokesperson is briefing now."

'Good morning, today we are going to try to answer your questions. The Surgeon General will be speaking here in a moment and will bring you up to speed with what is happening and the latest information about the virus from the CDC. But first let me start with a statement from the White House.'

'President Wilson has been fully apprised of the situation in Madagascar and has directed the NSC to gather as much human intelligence as possible in Africa and Australia. We are at this moment putting eyes on the ground. President Wilson was forced to dismiss the head of the CIA and the Secretary of Defense this morning because of their failure to have proper oversight of intelligence sources during this outbreak. He

views that lack of control as a dereliction of duty on the part of those entrusted to provide our security. President Wilson has named Asst SecDef Johnson as acting SecDef and has nominated Senator Umbridge from Tennessee as the next head of the CIA. Since congress is not in session President Wilson has used his executive authority to appoint Umbridge as acting director effective immediately. The President has entrusted the Surgeon General as coordinating authority in all efforts related to the containment of the Marionette virus. The President has great faith in Surgeon General Camer to ensure that the American people remain safe from harm.'
'That concludes the statement from the White House. Now the Surgeon General will make a statement and answer questions.'

***

Camer was a former doctor at Walter Reed. He had been the right doctor to the right people. He wasn't a bad doctor. He was actually pretty good, but this position was supposed to be mostly ceremonial without any real authority. The President had just changed that and now the nation was waiting hear what the man who was now supposed to fix this had to say.

***

"Good morning. Let me begin with New York City. Yesterday afternoon there was a reported case of Marionette virus in an apartment complex on Long Island. The supposed infected patient was a newly arrived visitor from France here with his wife to visit their daughter and grandchild. They arrived yesterday, and he began showing symptoms this morning. His family had found him unresponsive and called 911 assuming he had suffered a heart attack. When paramedics arrived, they reported that the patient had resumed respiration but was unresponsive to stimuli. That was the last report from the paramedic unit. The apartment complex has been quarantined and the residents are being told to shelter in place. We are attempting to gather more information about the travels of the couple prior to their arrival and we are also attempting to contact anyone who was on their flight from France. Thus far those contacted have shown no sign of infection. We are classifying this as a potential pandemic as we expect this to become more widespread. We do not have mortality rates yet but we believe they are higher than we would like to see. We are continuing to develop information about this virus and we will continue to update the American people. At this time we are advising all businesses to consider skeleton crews and for most people to remain close to their homes unless immediate needs arise. The US government will remain staffed but we are declaring that all non-essential personnel to be furloughed until further notice. We will remain vigilante. Questions?"

***

"Shit" JW said under his breath turning down the radio. "I think we need to skip the burger and head on home." He called Kate.

Kate had just started browning the meat when her phone rang.

"Where are you?" Kate sounded strained.

"We should be there in about thirty minutes. I left my truck, I'll tell you all about it when we get home. How are you doing?"

"I am better now, I just wish you were here." Kate did not sound relaxed.

"Be there soon, love ya" JW hit the end button and started flipping through his contacts again.

Kate walked into the living room and turned the sound down on the TV. The images were jumping between street cameras and phone video interrupted briefly by one talking head after another.

Bridger was stubbing out his fourth cigarette and lighting his fifth. He had spent the last twenty minutes on the phone with the newly promoted deputy post commander at Ft. Bragg, who just happened to be his last commanding officer in the 82nd Airborne when Bridger was finishing out his contract. Colonel Eckerd, oops, General Eckerd had told him just about the same thing he heard in the last three calls he placed. Nobody knew anything for sure except that there were places they were talking to a few hours ago that they couldn't talk to now. There are whole parts of nations just going dark. They are trying to figure out if they are having communications issues or lost power or just what the hell was going on. The conversations all told him one thing for sure. There was a lot of confusion about exactly what was happening.

He stood there smoking and thinking. Downtown Nashville is a beautiful place. It invites people to stroll the streets and wander down by the river. He was about a block from Broadway and he wondered if going into a bar at 9:30 in the morning and having a couple of shots would raise any eyebrows. He started walking.

The morning was in full swing and some folks were standing outside out their workplaces enjoying the morning sun. The day was warming up nicely from a cool start. It was the first really cool morning that had a good north wind with it. The blustery air made folks stand a little closer to the buildings, and he was able to navigate the sidewalks without too much interference. He made a right-hand turn away from the river he had been strolling beside and started up Broadway. He turned right again into *The Oasis*. The guy behind the bar looked back over his shoulder away from the TV that he and the rest of the folks in the bar were watching and asked Bridger,

"What can I get for ya?"

"Too early for tequila?"

"Hell no man, according to the TV, right now seems like the perfect time for tequila!"

"Serve it up." He said as he sat down at the bar.

The other folks there appeared to be the live act that played the day shift. A guy from Georgia, another from South Carolina and the singer trekked all the way from California and looked like he wanted to be the new Garth Owens or somebody, Bridger didn't really get country music. He was listening to them discuss the news. One said he read online that if you get infected, you start trying to eat other people. Another one said the brain shuts down and people just wonder around. What was obvious to Bridger was that nobody here really knew what was going on. He wondered if that was true everywhere. He looked up at the newscast. His phone rang.

"JW, I am amazed at your timing," he said

"What do you mean?" JW said as he sat in the passenger seat of Josh's SUV.

"Well I was just wondering if anybody knew what was going on, and you call."

"You have got to be kidding, tell me you know

something about this. How bad is this going to be?" JW starred out the window, beginning to get a nervous feeling in his gut.

"JW, I have talked to several people including Mike Eckerd, he's deputy Post CO at Bragg now, and they all tell me the same thing. They don't know shit, but they all paint the same picture. Area reports infection, area urgently calls for help, and area goes dark. And it all happens within hours. I don't KNOW what this is, but it doesn't matter at this point. If this thing gets going, it doesn't stop. I am about one drink away from getting in my car and coming down to hook up with you." Bridger was almost sure he had made that decision already.

"We'll have that drink together, when you get here," JW said, wishing the drive from Nashville to South Springs was a lot less than five hours.

"JW, I am serious. I am about to get in my car, stop by my house, get my big bag of guns, my bulk box of ramen and my secret spy compass I got in my cereal box and head your way." Now Bridger knew he had the makings of a plan.

"I'll keep the beer cold." JW said.

"Brother I am on my way" Bridger downed his drink and stood up.

"Fellas, y'all have a great day" he exited the bar and headed back the way he came.

When he got to his townhouse he changed out of his suit and put on some jeans and a shirt. He headed to the kitchen to see what kind of supplies he had because he did not intend to stop on his trip. Was he really going to do this? Load up and head south to see a guy he hadn't spoken to in years just because they happen to be both nervous about the same thing. If it were anybody other than JW Toles, the answer would be obvious. Since it was JW, the answer was pretty obvious too. He started pulling cans off the shelf.

Josh and JW had about five miles to go,

they came to the main intersection on 44. If they turned left, they would find themselves headed to the highway and the big bridge over the river. Continuing straight would take them across the river on the old two-lane bridge and on down 44 to the turn into their neighborhood. Josh went straight. When they crossed the bridge JW briefly came out of his thoughts to notice Kate's school. It looked all nice and neat. The buses parked in the parking lot all lined up just waiting to bring the kids back. All the playground equipment stood perfectly still, anticipating the end of the fall break. JW went back to thinking.

Kate opened the pantry and grabbed the beans. She was headed to the fridge to get the tomatoes when Scott yelled out.

"Mom, come in here, now!"

Kate went into Scott's room and he had a live stream running on his main viewer. It was chaos. People running. There were people down on the ground and people leaning over them, a lot of people leaning over them.

"I don't want to see anymore of this stuff from Spain, Scott." Kate said turning back

"Mom, that's Atlanta!"

Kate stopped.

JW and Josh turned into the driveway. As they pulled into the garage JW got out and looked back down the driveway. Standing on the front porch across the street was Evelyn Collins. Evelyn was the only other person still living in the cul-de-sac that was here when JW and Kate moved in. There were five houses in the cul-de-sac and four of them had been bought during the downturn. One was JW's but the other three had been speculators who sold them at the first chance they got to make a profit. Since then they had been bought and sold a few more times. Evelyn and Max Collins had been living here when JW and Kate moved in. Right now two houses were for sale and empty, the latest just two weeks ago when Ray and Margie Dockery

moved out and headed to Ray's new job in
Huntsville. The other one, Joe Strong's house,
had been empty for about three years. Which
leads back to Evelyn Collins, sort of. Evelyn was
a year or two younger than JW but she carried
herself like she was much older. She was a
widow. A young widow by most standards. Her
husband, Max, had died in a freak hunting
accident. He and Joe Strong had gone duck
hunting with a few other guys. Somehow Max
fell out of the boat and his waders filled up with
water. He drowned. Joe had told JW once that
when Max went in the water his waders got so
heavy they couldn't pull him out. Joe said they
got him within an inch of the surface and he
could see Max desperately trying to reach his
neck out to get his mouth above water, but he
couldn't. Joe said he watched the light go out
right there one inch below the surface. Joe had
moved out about three months later and his
house still sat empty. JW wondered if Evelyn
had ever heard that part. It wasn't something
you brought up on a casual hello at the mailbox.

The only other neighbor on the street was Carlos
and Rosita Menendez. They had been living here
about three years. Carlos was a professor at the
University and Rosita was a pediatric nurse.
They had left two days earlier heading to Disney
with their son and his family. So for right now
Evelyn and the Toles were the only people in the
cul-de-sac.

Bridger was a firm believer in the 2nd
Amendment. He actually had a big bag of guns.
He decided in his mind that he was going to fully
commit to this being a full-blown Armageddon
event and he was going to be armed to the teeth.
If it turned out to be a false alarm, oh well. It was
always fun to get all his guns out. He loaded the
bag into the trunk of his car. He carried a pistol
on his hip and he had another stuffed into the
glove box. He loaded a backpack with a days
worth of food and water into the passenger seat
and he put a box with more supplies in the back
seat. He knew he would stop and get gas at the

station right down from the house. He was ready to go. He walked back inside to see if there was anything else he needed. Bridger never married. Never had kids. Never wanted to. For times just like this.

"Nope, got everything I need." He locked the door, chuckled, and got in his car.

He pulled into the gas station. There were several cars getting gas, and he put his credit card in the terminal to start his pump. As he stood there pumping he looked around. He made eye contact with a few of the other patrons and he saw a look he had seen before. Whenever they were in some shithole village in some shithole country and the bad guys were planning an attack, word would begin to spread through the town. Usually the moments before an attack, the locals would have this look. Anticipation of annihilation is what JW had called it. Bridger was seeing that look right now.

An explosion broke through the sky. It

wasn't close enough for him to fear the effects
but it was close enough that he felt them. His
body vibrated and his ears registered the
pressure change. He brought his shoulder up
around his neck and bent his knees. The sky
darkened with a smoke cloud to his north
towards the river. He had put 11 gallons into his
tank. Bridger decided that was exactly enough.
He dropped the nozzle back into the slot and
pulled away without getting a receipt. He
processed the quickest route south and turned
left then right then left again. He was trying not
to act like he was running for his life, but there
was a nagging feeling up the back of his neck
that he needed to go faster. He made a right and
headed for the on-ramp to I-65 south. He didn't
see the man until he had made contact with him.
The guy just (fell?) walked right in front of him
as he went under the bridge. He slammed on the
brakes. He jumped out. What he expected to see
was someone broken to bits with bones sticking
out everywhere, which is what he saw. What he
didn't expect was to see him trying to get back

up.

"Hey, hey stop. Sit back down. Let me help."
Bridger said, "I am so sorry, I didn't see you."

But the man just continued to try to stand. Both his legs were broken below the knee, typical in a car strike. The right leg had broken cleanly and was only partially attached; the bones were sticking out, just like the bones of his wrist. He kept trying to swing his leg back under him and every time he did the foot and ankle swung awkwardly away. He would fall forward bracing himself on the bones sticking out of his wrist. He never cried out in pain or said a word. The asphalt had torn his face and his nose was gone. A flap of skin that had torn off his forehead covered one eye and the whole right side of his face was a streak of blood and skin. His left eye settled on Bridger. He was dumbstruck. The good eye, well better eye, was opaque. He could tell that it was looking at him. He saw the expression of the man's face change when the eye settled on him. It turned angry. The man (thing) doubled his effort to stand. Bridger stopped. He stood there for a second processing what he was seeing. He squinted and turned his head sideways.

"Was this it? Is this Marionette? Here, right here." He decided he would get in his car and dial 911 and wait for an ambulance. He hit send. No service. He hit send again. No service. The man outside was now unable to do anything more than just drag himself on his stumps and was dragging as hard as he could, blood trailing behind. His better eye never leaving Bridger.

"Screw it, if it's not zombies, they'll just have to get me for hit and run." he said, putting the car in reverse and backing away. He pulled back out into the road and watched as the man he had hit, broken legs and arms and all, desperately tried to crawl down the street after him.

He jumped up on the interstate and set off at 83 miles per hour. In his rear-view mirror were the tops of tall buildings in the distance peaking from behind the trees. Bridger turned his attention forward. The sign said Birmingham 188 miles. The traffic going south was a little heavier than normal for a lunchtime rush but not much. It was just past 1:30 and he went faster. He decided the state troopers would have better things to do in the apocalypse than give him a speeding ticket. He pressed the accelerator further. He was faster than most of the traffic but again, not by much. He passed a few minivans and SUV's that looked like they were headed camping or to the beach but when he looked at the driver, he saw confusion. He felt like he was trying to outrun something. As though all the bad stuff was behind him but gaining.

Together

When JW and Josh walked through the back door, Kate for the first time since JW left yesterday, felt a little better. They had been through a lot together. It was hard to make a marriage work. They loved each other desperately and had since the first moment they met. It made the difficult parts that much harder. Sometimes love isn't enough. They had crossed that bridge a time or two but every time they decided that whatever they had to do, they had to be together. It was that unyielding desire to be together that made them do the hard work. She hugged him tight.

"I am glad you're home, what happened to your head?" Kate asked

"Nothing, it isn't important anymore. We have to talk. SCOTT get in here." Yelling towards the bedroom.

Scott came in and sat down at the kitchen table. They all sat.

"I talked to Bridger again, he is headed this way." JW said.

The look on Kate's face told JW that she understood immediately the seriousness of what he had just said. If Bridger Preston is dropping whatever a 45-year-old single straight bachelor has to drop and coming down here to see him, it means Bridger is worried. Kate started to worry again.

"It should take Bridger about five or six hours to get here. That puts us after dark." JW said. "Scott I need you to give me a breakdown of what you know so far."

"Well we just saw some video out of Atlanta and it looks bad. I have seen video from New York,

Boston, Washington DC, Philadelphia, Raleigh, Cleveland and Minneapolis. I have seen images and read stories from all over the West Coast and Canada. It's all the same. People are attacking other people. The military and police can't seem to stop it and it is spreading fast. It started showing up yesterday morning on some gamer YouTube channels out of Australia and Madagascar. It looked like the same thing only shot from different angles so everybody started calling bullshit. Sorry." He continued "Yesterday when I called you into my room it had started showing up again, only this time it was on more 'newsy' type channels with a LOT more footage. In a little over 24 hours it went from a few random places in Madagascar to all over the world. What are the next 24 hours going to be like?" Scott asked, not because he expected an answer but because started doing the math in his head.

JW was looking down while Scott was talking; he had started to do the math too, he just kept looking at a little scratch on the top of the kitchen table, he spoke.

"Listen guys," hardly believing what he was about to say. "We need to make a decision and make it now. We know whatever this is it spreads fast and brings bad things with it. From what we have seen, and I am not saying it is 100% true, the 'infected' are not in control of their own actions. That makes them dangerous. We don't know how this is spread but we have to make a couple of assumptions. Contact with the 'infected' is bad. People are going to panic. We are going to protect ourselves and we are not going to lose our heads. The next few days we'll see what happens but I think we need to be a little more proactive."

They were all nodding.

"Ok, Josh, you and Scott start emptying some of those plastic totes we keep the Christmas stuff in and start putting canned goods in them, if we have to leave we need to have some things ready to go." JW said.

"What do you want us to do with the Christmas stuff?" Josh asked.

"Just dump it out in the storage building, I don't think we are going to be decorating this year." JW said.

Up until this very moment Josh had not contemplated what was really happening. He knew this was serious but really, how serious is some virus. Yes everybody gets all nervous, then they get their shots, and everybody moves on. He looked around the table and the faces of his parents told him, this was not going to be easy or short or over soon. For the first time he could remember, he felt unprepared. He was seventeen, invincible and had everything in front of him. He realized now that the future he always envisioned for himself may not turn out that way.

"Kate, we need to go have a conversation with Evelyn Collins." JW said starting to get up from the table.

Kate stood joining him as they started towards the front door.

"Y'all boys get that stuff packed up, we'll be right back. Then you and I, Josh, may have an errand to run. Maybe you too Scott." JW said walking out the door.

Kate and JW walked out the front door and JW started down the sidewalk when Kate touched his arm. He paused, turning back to look.

"Why do we need to see Evelyn?" Kate asked

"I have an idea about making this place just a little more secure and I want to make sure she would be ok with it. And if she isn't, to let her know that I am doing it, anyway. If I can figure out how." JW turned and started walking. Kate followed.

When JW and Kate returned, Josh noticed his mother had this odd look of shock and humor on her face. When his father started explaining his plan, Josh had the same look.

"We are going to steal two school buses from your mother's school." JW said.

Scott was the only one to laugh out loud. Josh wanted to at first but when he looked at his father, he knew it was not a joke. Not even close.

"I can get into the school and get the keys out of the office." Kate volunteered because she had heard the whole plan across the street at Evelyn Collins house.

"Ok, I think we should plan ongoing as soon as possible. I also think would all should go to the school together. Well, not Evelyn, but all four of us. I am going to drive one of the buses and your mother will drive the other. But first let's head out into my room." JW said.

JW had a small four by four room in the garage that was mainly for the hot water heater but he had wedged his gun safe into it when they first moved in. He wasn't a gun nut or a prepper so he didn't have an arsenal. The gun safe did hold several handguns, 9mm mostly, which is what he really enjoyed shooting. He had his new rifle and three pump shotguns. He also had his deer rifle and a couple of old 30/30 lever action rifles from his grandfather. He grabbed the lever actions. He also grabbed a box of shells and one of his 9MM pistols. He turned and handed the rifles to Josh.

"Load some rounds into these two." JW passed that ammunition.

"Kate, I want you to carry this." He handed Kate the 9MM, it was in a holster with a clip on it so she could just slide the clip inside her waistband. She knew how to use the gun too.

"Scott, you and Josh will carry these rifles but they will stay in your mother's vehicle. As will you. When we get there your mother and I will get two buses started and I will lead us back in one bus, you (nodding to Josh) and your brother will follow in your mother's car. Your mother brings up the rear in the other bus."

They all loaded up into Kate's SUV and started to pull out. JW hit the button on the garage door. As they headed out the long road through their neighborhood, JW continued the plan.

"Once we are moving, I really don't want to stop. There are three stop signs and one traffic light between the school and here. They are all suggestions at this point. If I don't stop, you don't stop. Stay tucked in tight. As long as we stay tight we should be fine." He continued. "Once we get back to the neighborhood we are going to park them at the entrance to the cul-de-sac. If we pull both of them back into the wood off the curb on either side they should cover the entrance. It won't keep anyone out on foot that really wants to get in, but it may discourage folks who aren't looking to put in any effort. And it will definitely keep other vehicles from getting all the way back here before realizing there is only one way out of the neighborhood."

The way the cul-de-sac was positioned was an afterthought. The original plan had houses rounding each corner coming out of the cul-de-sac but they never got built. The main road ends and the cul-de-sac is simply a street that goes slightly down hill off to the right at a 45-degree angle from the dead end. Trees line the entrance two lots deep on both sides. The pseudo isolation is what drove JW's interest in the first place.

When they arrived at Kate's school they pulled around behind the buses.

Kate and JW got out quickly entered the school to retrieve the keys. They chose two buses from the rear line. JW got into the first bus and started it. He went back out. Kate had started the other bus and joined him. They all four stood together at the back of the two running school buses and realized they were about to commit grand theft auto of government property. If it wasn't the zombie apocalypse, they were going to have some very serious explaining to do.

"Stay tight. I will back out, then Josh you get behind me. I will wait until your mother flashes her headlights and then we go. Stay tight." JW said. "If something happens and we get separated. Get back home."

They froze. The approaching sound of sirens made them think their heist was over before it got started. But four police cars, a fire truck and two more ambulances raced by headed towards the highway. They looked at each other again. It was time to go. JW backed his bus out and Josh fell in behind him as he pulled towards the exit of the parking lot. He waited for Kate to fall in behind Josh. She flashed her headlights. Off they went. As he went through the first stop sign without stopping, he saw a few folks gathered in their yards talking to each other. At the next non-stop sign, he saw another group of folks standing outside the church on the corner. Nobody seemed to notice the two school buses rolling down the street. Why would they? The light was green and they went right through. The next intersection was the four-way where they would turn right into their neighborhood. As JW turned in his heart leapt into his throat. There was a sheriff's car parked at the intersection. The driver's door was open but JW didn't see anyone. He didn't hang around and look. He headed towards the back of the neighborhood. The rest of the caravan followed.

Bridger was about 30 miles north of Birmingham and traffic had definitely picked up. The northbound lane out of Birmingham was packed with cars leaving town and Bridger began to think he might need to bypass the city. He took the next exit and pulled into a gas station to check the map on his phone. No service. He looked up at the service station and wondered if they still sold maps. They did. He got back in his car and opened up the map. He found the road he was currently on and traced it to where it intersected another county road that headed south. He pulled away. Twelve miles down the road he came to County Rd 6. He turned south. He knew he could stay on 6 until he crossed County Rd 81. He could stay on 6 to Northview and get back on the main highway to South Springs or he could turn onto 81 for a few miles and hit 44 and head straight to JW's house. He would take 44. He turned on the radio and was surprised the XM station he usually tuned to, Rock Plaza Central, was broadcasting news.

***

'The Federal Emergency Management under the Direction of the Surgeon General has issued a shelter-in-place warning for all citizens East of the Mississippi River to include the entire Ohio River Valley. A state of emergency now exists in all major metropolitan areas and the President has activated ALL National Guard personnel to respond to the crises. The governors of the individual states are now entrusted with plenary powers from the federal government to oversee coordinated efforts related directed to their states. FEMA stands by to offer any assistance to the governors.'

***

Bridger thought that had been a long-winded way of saying you're on your own. And he finally decided that whatever *this* was, it was going to get worse before it gets better. He picked up the pace.

He had just turned south onto 44 when he saw the wreck. A log-truck had spilled its load right on top of a car. The cab of the truck had detached from the hauler and was off the road slammed into a tree. He stopped the car and got out. The vehicle under the logs was crushed. He looked in through what he thought was the drivers window. He heard shuffling in the dark opening. Suddenly a young woman appeared in the window.

"Help me, my husband and I are trapped and he is knocked out or something."

"Ok, ok, let me see what I can do." He said.

He surveyed the situation and figured he could use his car to push the log blocking the window off and maybe get a space big enough for them to crawl out. He pulled his car up and started nudging the end of the log and finally got it to move the right way. He pushed it off and got out of his car. By the time he got back over to her car the woman was already crawling out. She put her feet on the ground and reached back in.

"Here let me help", Bridger said arriving by her side.

The young man was now awake but very disoriented. They coaxed him through the window. Bridger helped them over to the side of the road as another car pulled up. The old man got out and walked up to Bridger.

"Damn, what happened here?" he asked

"Don't know, just got here myself and helped these two out of the car." Bridger replied.

"Anybody check on the driver yet?" the man asked. It was the first time Bridger had thought about it.

"Not yet."

"Well y'all stay here and let me go check on him and we'll see if we can't get some help coming. My phone isn't working, can't get a signal but we'll figure it out." The old man started up the slope towards the cab of the truck. Bridger looked at his phone. It had been doing the tail chase emblem most of the way down. He was...

"Aahhhhhhhhahhhh" came a scream from the direction of the cab.

Bridger and the young woman ran up the little slope and stepped over to the driver's side. They were not prepared for what they saw.

The old man was on the ground, his face frozen in a scream that was no longer making any sound because the driver was currently ripping his throat out with his teeth. Blood was spraying everywhere and the driver was making guttural animal sounds as he slurped and chewed. The girl screamed. The driver raised his head slowly and turned to face them. His left arm had been deboned. All the skin and muscle was in a ball around his wrist and his arm was a collection of bone and sinew hanging down by his side since there was no muscle to move it any more. His face had been smashed against the steering wheel and one of his eyes was hanging out of its socket. One side of his mouth had been ripped open and his lower jaw was exposed. It was full of blood and flesh from the old man. He slowly tried to stand, as if trying to detect which way gravity was pulling him down and counteracting it. He was having difficulty getting up because he couldn't use his left arm.

"Stop dude" Bridger said. The young lady was in shock and froze. The driver stood.

"Stop now" Bridger summoned his most don't screw with me voice.

The driver started walking towards the girl. Bridger saw the same gait he had witnessed at the TV station on the bank of TVs. It was here. Now. He slid his pistol out of his hip holster and thumbed the safety. He raised it at the driver.

"Stop now or I WILL shoot you."

The driver never stopped. He was just a few feet from the girl. She had finally snapped too and was backpedaling away.

"Stop" He didn't stop.

Bridger fired one round into the man's right shoulder. He flinched from the impact but his gait never broke. Bridger fired again. Left shoulder. Same result.

He fired a third round. Center mass. He knew he had just blown this mans heart to pieces and yet the gait never changed. He was still moving when Bridger fired the fourth shot. Just over the right eye. The man went down.

"Shit." Bridger stood with his gun pointed at the

heap on the ground, fully expecting it to get back up again.

When he was sure it wasn't moving, he holstered his weapon and turned to look at the girl. She had gone to her knees. She had her hands over her ears and her mouth was agape. Her eyes met Bridger's.

"Holy fucking shit mister, what the fuck was that?" Bridger liked her instantly.

"I don't know. I think he had Marionette. I think that was what that was." motioning towards the lump on ground.

"Oh, shit, oh shit oh shit, what the fuck I mean what the literal fuck."

Bridger knew she was still in shock and she was starting to meltdown.

"Hey, hey we're ok. It's ok." He tried.

"OK? YOU JUST FUCKING SHOT A FUCKING MAN WHO WOULDN'T QUIT FUCKING

TRYING TO FUCKING ATTACK, EAT, RAPE, I
DON'T KNOW WHAT THE FUCK HE WAS
DOING BUT YOU KEPT FUCKING SHOOTING
HIM AND HE KEPT FUCKING MOVING EVEN
AFTER YOU FUCKING SHOT HIM, AND YOU
THINK IT'S OK?"

"Well when you put it like that." Bridger said.

He just stood there looking at her waiting
for the next flurry of "fuck" but she actually
laughed a little.

"Hey, what the hell is going on?" Bridger and the
girl looked back towards the road to see her
husband stumbling up towards them.

She stood and walked towards him
motioning for him to stay where he was. He
stopped. Bridger took one more look at the scene
in front of him. Two people had died right here.
Apparently one of them, twice. He turned to join
the couple by the road.

JW stood with his back to the cul-de-sac watching Kate get out of the bus she had just parked. It was parked nose to tail from the one JW had just parked. JW had pulled his into the woods just a little and Kate had parallel parked between the end of JW's bus and the woods behind her. She had to run over a few of the smaller pine trees to wedge it in tight.

"OK, I think that will do what we need." JW said.

Josh and Scott were already back inside the house and had gone to Scott's room to try to see if there was any more information. Scott clicked on the FEMA website. The normal splash page had been changed.

■■ ■ ı

***

A SHELTER IN PLACE ORDER IS IN EFFECT

"FEMA is now being directed at the state level. The Federal Emergency System has been fully activated. All coordination for assistance and evacuations should be directed to the respective state emergency management systems.

***

He clicked on the CNN link and it was completely down. As he started looking through all the news links, he would find some down, probably overwhelmed, and some had quit updating their content. Information, it seemed, was becoming the latest victim of Marionette. He began looking at social media. There was a lot more information, but he had always viewed it as mostly made up crap. He decided that under the circumstances he would be more open-minded. He found a lot of videos of folks seemingly infected by Marionette, and he also found a lot of conspiracy theories. Some said it was an attack by aliens, some by Bigfoot and an interesting one about global warming releasing ancient bacteria. The one video that got his attention showed a girl on the ground with someone biting her leg. She was screaming and when they finally got the biter off her, she scrambled back away. As the camera turned from the biter, lying on the ground dead after being hit in the head with a shovel, to the girl it shows her face and as you watch, her eyes go opaque and she bites the arm of the guy who is carrying her. The person operating the camera screams and takes off but as they put the phone to their side to run, you can see the girl continuing to bite (eat) the guy's arm.

Josh looked away from the monitor briefly to see JW standing in the doorway.

His mouth was open and Josh thought he saw, for the first time, fear wash over his Dad's face. It was almost immediately replaced with a face Josh had seen all his life. The face he had seen when he and Josh were on the way to the hospital when Josh broke his leg. The face he had seen when Scott had that incident with the butcher knife that cost Scott the tip of his pinky. The face he had seen his dad make to his mother when they were struggling with money. The face that said, don't worry, I will take care of it. Josh began to wonder if that face he had always seen as reassuring was just a mask. In that moment, he looked just a little smaller to Josh.

Scott turned around and asked.

"What do you think, Josh?" he asked, seeing his father standing in the doorway.

"Hey Dad, did you see that?" Scott asked.

JW answered.

"I saw it, I think we need to start thinking about what we do next." he said.

"JOHN get out here now." Kate yelled.

All three ran out the front door, half expecting to see her down on the ground being attacked just like the girl in the video. Instead, Kate was standing in the street pointing back up towards the top of the hill where they had just parked the buses.

"There is someone up there walking around the

buses." Kate said.

From their angle looking back up towards the buses, which were about 100 yards away, they could see a set of legs walking on the other side. It looked like dark pants with dark shoes.

"I bet it's the deputy. I better go up there." JW started walking. Josh fell in beside him. Kate and Scott waited. JW and Josh wedged themselves between the buses but when they got through they didn't see anyone at first, then they saw the deputy standing up the road. They walked a few steps towards the deputy and called out but the deputy was focused on the house up the road and had started walking towards it. Josh ran on ahead a few steps. JW thought to himself that the deputy was being really cautious about where he was looking. The deputy was bent over a little as he walked forward and JW thought it made the deputy looked like he was shuffling. Josh was reaching out to get the deputies attention. Shuffling, shuffling. JW quit thinking. The gun was out and the round had already slammed into the back of the deputy's head before Josh ever touched him. JW stood there, wisps of smoke coming from the end of the Ruger, and started shaking. He managed to thumb the safety back on and holster the gun before he threw up. Barely.

"Jesus Dad, Jesus. You just killed him. You just killed a cop. Are you out of your mind?" Josh was screaming at JW. JW, for his part, was doubled over trying to figure out why lunch came before breakfast. Josh kept yelling and backing up towards the buses. Kate pushed through just as Josh reached the bus.

"What happened, are you ok, where is your father, was that a gunshot?" Kate fired questions at Josh, who was still yelling towards back towards his father. She could see JW up the road a little doubled over.
"He just shot him. He just blew his head off. He's crazy mom. I think he snapped. He just shot him." Josh finally answered her.

Kate started walking towards JW. He glanced up and saw her coming and stood. She raised her arms up slightly, palms down, letting JW know to just calm down. He got the message. She walked up to him and hugged him. She wasn't quite sure what happened, but she had actually seen him snap once. This wasn't what it looked like. At least not the vomit.

"Hey, hey. It's ok. What happened?" she asked.

"I shot him. I think he was one of those things. He wouldn't answer, he just kept walking. Josh was reaching for him. I...I..." he trailed off.

"John, *was* he one of those things? Was he?" she begged.

JW looked at her, eyes red rimmed and bloodshot and tears slowly coming down his cheek.

"I don't know" he collapsed to his knees. She went down with him.

Bridger knelt down beside the couple as they sat down on one of the logs scattered across the road. Cars pulled up to the wreck, but they were all hesitant to try to get around it. As they quickly u-turned to find another route Bridger could see the faces in the cars. It was panic.

"Listen, I don't know what is going on, but I don't think any help is coming." He started.

"I think we all are going to be on our own for a while. My name is Bridger, Bridger Preston." He extended his hand towards the couple. The man took his hand off his head and shook it.

"Raj Varma. This is my wife, Tilly." He said. Nodding towards the girl Bridger had just (saved?) helped.

"We were trying to get back to South Carolina." Raj continued.

"And now our car is a fucking pancake." Tilly chimed in.

Bridger didn't know what to do. He

wasn't about to turn around and head back north but he didn't want to just leave these folks on the side of the road.

"Listen, I can't help you get to Carolina but I have a friend a little ways south of here that will let you stay with him until we can figure it out. I don't know if that would help or not but I am offering to let you go with me to South Springs."

The two looked at each other. Tilly spoke.

"Mister."

"Bridger." he interrupted

"Bridger, mister, whatever. After what the fuck I just saw back there, I don't give a rats ass if you are going to Eastbumfuck Egypt, just take us the fuck with you." She said.

"She gets going when she gets nervous." Raj said.

"Yeah, I caught that." He said.

"Fuck you both." Tilly stood.

"Are you sure we'll be safe going to South Springs?" He asked.

"Raj, I don't know if we'll be safe walking over there and getting your stuff out of your car, but I guess we'll find out." He said.

They all stood and walked over to the crushed car. They could get to the back seat which allowed them to pull some of their things from the trunk. Raj and Tilly were on a belated honeymoon in New Orleans so they had a few suitcases of clothes and not much else. They hadn't exactly planned for the end of the world. They loaded the things they had into the trunk of Bridger's car. Tilly got in the front seat so Raj could lie down in the back. They slowly wound their way around the scattered logs and came out the other side heading south on 44 again. It had started to get dark. Bridger could see the lights from a gas station. Raj was resting across the back seat. As they passed the station, the lights flickered out and back on again. They kept driving. Raj started talking.

"Back there, at the wreck, we had left New Orleans this morning trying to get back home. The interstate was very busy and we got caught in a traffic jam. We got off the interstate and had started going on the back roads. The phones quit working and we had pulled over to try to figure out which way to go. The truck just came around the corner and turned over on us. We were just sitting there." He trailed off.

"Do you know what is happening?" Tilly asked.

Bridger was caught off guard because she hadn't used fuck every third word.
"Not sure, but I have seen a lot of the same kind of things from video's of this Marionette virus going around."

"Yeah, you already said that, but I asked if you knew what the fuck is happening?" There she was. "I mean why the fuck is the radio only playing that stupid FEMA warning and nothing else? Why don't our phones work? Why are the lights flickering? I mean a fucking virus doesn't make the fucking phones quit working? It's obviously not a fucking computer virus, so I'll ask you again, do you know what the fuck is happening?" she spoke the last line somewhat mockingly for someone who had just been saved by the guy she was mocking, Bridger thought.

"No. I don't know for sure but I can make a guess, that's what I do for a living, make guesses. My guess is that this virus is making people panic, and possibly for good reason, and when people panic accidents happen. If those accidents affect the right power distribution sources, like say, a transmission line to a cell tower or twenty, then you have outages. If the folks who are supposed to fix those power disruptions and outages are also panicking, they aren't working. Things begin to break down. If the crisis passes, things get fixed. We are right now at the finding out if the crisis is going to pass stage. But that is just a guess." Bridger finished.

"Well that's fucking great." Tilly said as they

drove into the growing darkness.

Kate had managed to get JW back in the house. He was sitting in the living room leaned forward in his chair, hands crossed against his forehead like he was praying. Kate was trying to finish cooking, even though she knew nobody felt like eating. Josh had gone into Scott's room. Kate walked to the door.

"Josh, can we go outside and talk for a minute?" Just as she said that the lights flickered. "Crap." Scott said, as his monitors blinked and everything started rebooting.

"Sure, nothing to see here anyway." Josh said and followed her out.

They walked out onto the front porch, the sun was finishing its day and the sky had turned purple, Kate motioned for Josh to sit down in the swing with her. He sat.

"Josh, I don't know what you think happened up

there." Kate started.

"I know exactly what happened up there, Mom. He freaked. He shot the guy." Josh interrupted.

"He thought he was going to hurt you, he thought he was infected with this virus." Kate said.

"So because he thought the guy was infected, he shot him. What if he thinks I am infected or you or Scott, does he just shoot us?" Josh asked.

"That's different Josh, your father did what he did to protect you. Don't you see that?" Kate said.

"No mom, I don't see...what the hell?" Josh looked up the hill.

There was a woman squeezing between the buses. Josh looked past her and could see someone else trying to follow her. Kate turned. The woman fell down and screamed. They took off running towards the top of the road. The woman tried to get up. The other person made in through just as Josh and Kate got close. He fell on top of the woman. She screamed in pain. Kate and Josh stopped. They could see the man taking bites of skin off the woman's face. Every time its head lifted up a gush of blood would fill the hole it had made with its teeth. The woman was taking deep breaths between screams and trying to get free but with every move the gnashing jaws of her attacker would clamp down and she would scream again, it's hand digging into the flesh of her stomach and coming up bloody.

Josh looked down at his mother's hip and saw the gun she had been wearing since they stole the buses. He grabbed it out of the holster before Kate could stop him. He thumbed the safety and fired. The round hit the thing in the back. It looked up. The woman screamed and it went back to biting her in the chest. He fired again into its shoulder. It stood and turned towards Josh and Kate. They were standing about fifteen feet away. The woman had stopped screaming. He fired three more rounds haphazardly at it. The first shot hit its throat. The second shot hit it just under the eye and it went down. The third shot missed entirely. They stood there.

Kate slid past the body on the ground and went to the woman. She was dead. Kate closed the woman's eyes and walked back over to Josh. He was still pointing the gun at the pile in front of him. His eyes were wide.

"Hey, hey. You ok?" Kate asked a stupid question and knew it. "It's ok, honey. Just let me take the gun." He handed it over without a thought.

"Shit, mom. What was that?" Josh was starting to shake a little.

"I don't know son. I don't know." She turned to hug him.

As she did, she could hear...something. She looked back. The woman had raised her head. Kate stepped back, pulling Josh with her. He reached out and steadied her. The woman raised herself up onto her elbows and tried to sit up. Her ripped open abdomen didn't have the muscle left to sit up. Her legs twisted underneath and she rolled to one side. What guts were left inside her spilled out on the road. She managed to get her arms under her as she rolled over. She raised her face to them. Her eyes were opaque and her face was dripping blood out of each bite the thing had made. She looked at Kate and Josh and screeched.

Kate's face had contorted into a mix of fear and pity. The last expression was resolution. She raised the pistol she had taken from Josh. She shot the woman in the forehead. They stumbled back towards the house. Kate stopped.

"What?" Josh sounded exasperated.

"If those two can get through, others can too. We have to move the bus a little. Just a little. Just enough to close that gap." She said.

Her and Josh started back to the buses. They carefully walked around the two bodies now lying in the street. She climbed into the bus and put it in neutral. There was enough downhill slope that it rolled forward on its own until it touched the back of the other bus. She climbed back out.

They stood for a second. They were both trying to process what had just happened. Josh was wondering what they were going to do next. Kate was wondering what it was like on the other side of those buses. Evening had given way to the streetlamp. It flickered. They ran back to the house.

The Dying Fire

They had made good time down 44 and they were about forty miles from South Springs. Bridger had noticed that the traffic was starting to get a little heavier coming from the direction they were going. Most of the houses and businesses they passed had no lights. They hadn't passed anything in a while except pine trees and power poles.

"I have to pee." Tilly said, breaking the silence.

"I don't think there are any service stations nearby." Bridger said.

"I don't give a shit. Just stop the car and I can go

on the side of the road. I am about to burst." She
said.

Bridger saw a mailbox ahead and saw
that the mail truck had created a place to pull
over. He used it. He couldn't see any lights up
the dirt road from the mailbox.

"I think I'll go too while we are stopped." Raj
said, sitting up in the back seat now.

They had been listening to the radio in
the silence and the reporting had gone from
FEMA emergency broadcasts to individuals at
local stations reporting about local instances of
the virus. They had not picked up any stations
from South Springs yet but everything
everywhere else was sounding real bad. People
attacking people, police and military beginning
to be overwhelmed. Shelter location reports and
emergency contact information to help find
missing people.

Bridger got out and walked out into the
road. He scanned both directions and couldn't

see any other cars coming. Tilly had stepped out
and was crouching down just outside the car
with one hand on the handle for support. Raj
walked to the nearest tree just off the road. He
was looking back over his shoulder.

"How much longer until we get where we are
going?" he asked.

"Maybe another hour or so." Bridger replied.

Tilly and Raj were finished with their
business and leaned against the back of the car.
Tilly pulled a pack of cigarettes out of her pocket.
Raj looked at her disapprovingly.

"Oh fuck off." She said, as she lit the smoke.

Bridger walked to the back of the car.
Pulled out a cigarette of his own and lit it.

"Where are we going?" Raj asked.

Bridger turned to answer him but his
attention was drawn up the dirt road they were
currently blocking. Someone was running

towards them.

"Help, please. He's sick. Our power went out and we can't get the phones to work." The boy running towards them yelled.

"Who's sick? What's wrong with them?" Bridger asked as he stepped around Raj and met the boy in the dirt road.

"My grandpa, he's sick. He has heart problems and he isn't feeling good. We tried to call the ambulance like before but we can't get through." The breathless boy said.

"Who is, we?" Raj asked

Bridger looked back over his shoulder at Raj. Raj caught the look of approval.

"My mom and me. We came to check on him and he..." The boy ran out of breath.

"Ok, ok. Settle down. We will get in the car and drive up to the house. I don't know what help we can give but we'll see what we can do." Bridger said.

"Thanks" the boy said. They all got in the car.

"You know, my husband is a doctor." Tilly said.

It just occurred to Bridger that he two people he had been riding with for the last hour were absolute complete strangers. He knew almost nothing about them. He hadn't asked. And they hadn't volunteered. They had spent the majority of their time together in shock. They had just listened to the radio and drove. What little talk they had managed had only been in response to what they had heard on the radio. Small talk had gone away.

"No, I didn't know that." He said.

"Dermatologist." Raj added.

They drove up the dirt road about fifty yards and the house appeared in the moonlight off to the left. They stopped in front of it. Sitting under the carport was an old pickup truck. Behind it was parked a small red SUV. As they stopped, the boy opened the back door and ran towards the house. Bridger, Tilly and Raj got out and walked to the front door. On the porch was a swing with one side on the ground, the chain long broken. There was an old stuffed chair that looked rattier than the swing. Next to the chair was a small bucket filled with sand and cigarette butts. Bridger swung the storm door back and stuck his head in.

"Hey, anybody here?" he yelled.

A woman, who appeared to be in her mid-thirties, came out of the hallway in front of Bridger and motioned them in. She saw his gun on his hip, and flushed.

"Are you a cop?" she asked.

"No, mam but don't worry, it's only for protection." He said in his most calming voice.

"Do I know you?" she asked as she squinted her eyes, trying to see him a little better in the candlelight.

"I don't think so, but you may have seen me on TV." He said.

"That's it, you're Bridger Presley." She said.

"Preston. Yes." He said.

"Preston. Yes Preston. You are the guy who talks about the army stuff. My husband is in the Army reserves and I watch you when I can. He says you know what you're talking about. He watches you too. My name is Sally. Sally Forester." She extended her hand. He took it.

"Nice to meet you Sally, this is Tilly and Raj Varma. Raj is a doctor." Nodding towards the couple coming through the door behind him.

Raj and Tilly made for an odd couple even before the apocalypse. He looked like the Rhodes scholar he was. Buttoned down and neatly pressed. Even now. She had fire red hair cut in what used to be called a pixie cut, Sally didn't know what they called it now. She also had horn-rimmed black glasses with the most striking green eyes and was dressed like a hippie from Sally's childhood. Sally smiled.

They all stood in the living room. Candles lit the house and it cast shadows over the furniture. It was the living room of an old man. One chair pushed against the wall with a table next to it. There were several half-filled glasses sitting on the table and one closed book with a pair of reading glasses sitting on them. One wall had pictures of children and several pictures of one older lady. One of which showed her kissing the bald head of a bearded man. On the other wall was a big flat screen TV. It was dead.

"How is your father doing?" Raj asked.

"Why don't you come and tell me. He is resting now but if you would look at him, I would feel better." Sally said.

She turned back down the hallway. Raj looked at Tilly. She shrugged. He followed the woman down the hallway. Tilly and Bridger waited in the living room. Tilly sat down in the chair. Bridger found a spot on the floor and leaned his back against the wall. He pulled out his phone. Nothing. The power blinked back on.

"Hooray" the boy yelled as he came out of the kitchen. The power blinked off again.

"Shoot" the boy said dejectedly.

Tilly was smiling at the boy when the woman came back down the hallway. Raj came behind her. Tilly saw the look Raj gave to the boy, and she walked him back into the kitchen away from Raj and his mother. He went willingly.

"He's not doing well. His breathing is shallow," Raj said. "I don't know for sure that being in a hospital would do any good, and this isn't a hospital. I don't think he has long."

Sally was crying. She knew, but she didn't want to accept it. She went back into the back room. Raj and Bridger stood looking at each other. Raj walked into the kitchen and brought

Tilly and the boy back down the hallway after Sally. Bridger was left alone. He looked outside. He couldn't see shit. Tilly and the boy came back, the boy was crying.

"He said his goodbyes." Tilly said with a tear rolling down her cheek. The boy went into the kitchen.

After a while, Sally and Raj came out of the back and closed the door behind them.

"He's gone." Raj said.

They walked into the living room. Sally sat in the chair and sobbed. Tilly knelt down and hugged her. They all gathered around her with their heads bowed trying to help comfort this stranger. They stood there for a long time. Sally finally spoke.

"He was so stubborn. He wouldn't quit smoking. He said something was going to kill him anyway, he might as well enjoy what time he has." She chuckled through her tears.

"Thank you for being here. I know this is very strange, but today has been a very strange day." Sally said.

"No fucking shit. Sorry. So sorry." Tilly said.

The boy walked from behind Raj and sat down on Sally's lap. He was almost too big for laps but not quite. His mother hugged him.

"Why are you crying momma?" he asked.

"Pawpaw passed Jesse. He's gone." She said.

"Not yet momma, I heard him back there, up and walking plain as day." Jesse said.

"Jesse, that's just the wind. Pawpaw's gone. We watched him go." She said nodding towards Raj.

"He's walking around momma, come look." Jesse said and jumped off his momma's lap and ran towards the back of the house. Sally started after him. Raj was looking confused. He and Tilly made eye contact. Bridger watched as a thought washed over Raj's face, then Tilly's, then his.

"Wait" They yelled in unison. But the boy had already reached the door to the bedroom at the end of the hall.

Sally watched as her son, only nine, opened the bedroom door. The thing inside that had once been his grandfather grabbed him by the back of the head and snatched him up. Before the boy could even scream the thing had bitten his nose completely off and was already taking another bite from the boys face. Sally screamed and ran towards the thing she once called Daddy. As she grabbed for her son, the thing let go of him and grabbed her arms. As she struggled to hold on to her son, the thing spun her around and bit deeply into her shoulder. She screamed in pain. It took another bite further up her neck and the blood came out in violent splashes.

Raj ran down the hallway and into the room. He stopped. The thing was down on the floor eating the woman. Jesse had managed to crawl towards the door. Raj fell backwards when Jesse reached up. Bridger stepped between them. He could see that Jesse was seriously injured but still alive. He grabbed his hand and pulled him towards the hall. The thing had its head down and was focused on what it was currently doing. Bridger didn't know how long that was going to be so he didn't take any chances. He pulled out his weapon and fired one round. It slammed into the top of the things head. It fell backwards against the bed it had already died on once and died again. Raj had pulled Jesse back into the living room. Bridger checked on Sally. She was dead. He sat down with his back to the door looking over the carnage. He reached into his pocket and produced a cigarette. He lit it and let it hang off his lips. He inhaled through his mouth and out his nose. Once, twice. Sally's eyes opened. Bridger didn't see them open. He only saw her sit up. She was facing away from him.

"Sally?" he said, cigarette falling out of his

mouth. He was trying to get up when she twisted on her butt and threw herself back at him. He managed to stick a foot out and it caught her in the stomach. His foot sank deep into the opening. She spun and even though her intestines were hanging from his foot down to the floor, she reached out for him. He got his hands up and grabbed her arms just below the shoulder. Her mouth slammed shut inches from his face. She was trying to extend her jaw towards him when he flipped her off him and onto her back. He slammed her down several times banging her head against the hardwood and threw himself back away from her. He produced the firearm again and placed one just below her nose. She fell. The candle fell off the table onto her. It began to burn her hair. Bridger stood and stumbled towards the light in the living room. He found Raj and Tilly standing over Jesse. He was dead. Bridger walked up, still holding the pistol and shot the boy in the head. He walked out the front door. The fire began to catch in the back bedroom.

"What the hell was that?" Tilly asked chasing him out the door. Raj followed her looking back over his shoulder as the storm door shut behind him.

"She came back." Bridger said.

"Who? What the hell do you mean 'came' back?" she said.

"The woman, Sally, she was dead. She came back. Just like the old man. Just like the truck driver. Just like the boy would have. She came back and attacked me." He was still walking towards the car.

"Stop, just stop. What are you saying? That can't..." she trailed off, the truth of what she had seen twice with her own eyes hitting hard.

"And where we are going there is someone who knows how to deal with this?" Raj asked.

"Folks, I don't know if there is anybody anywhere who knows how to deal with *this*." Pointing back at the house. "But if there is one guy in the world who I would want to help me get through *this*, well let me just say. We are on the right road." Bridger started up the car. Raj and Tilly took one more look, flames starting to lick the roof from the back of the house. They got in the car.

JW sat in the living room with the emergency broadcast signal repeating over the TV. He ignored it. The message had been playing for over an hour. It said the same thing. All JW heard was noise. Scott was in his room watching cellphone video being broadcast from all over the country. They all looked the same. It was horrific. The front door slammed open and Josh came into his room. Kate ran into the living room and turned the TV off. JW looked up at her.

"Whatever it is you think you have to deal with, deal with it. We need you here. Now."

She relayed the story of what had just happened

to her and Josh. By the time she had finished Josh and Scott had come into the living room.

"Dad, I'm sorry. I didn't get it, I do now." Josh said.

The lights went out. They didn't come back on. Kate found her way into the kitchen and grabbed a flashlight. She came back into the living room and lit candles. JW took the flashlight and walked out into the garage. He came back in with several more flashlights from his hunting bag. He gave one to Josh and one to Scott. He went into the bedroom and brought back the rifles he had given them earlier.

"From this moment forward, nobody leaves this house without being armed." He said flatly.

"Your mother and I are going to go and get Evelyn and bring her over here if she will come."

"What do we do?" Scott asked.

"Absolutely nothing."

JW and Kate walked out the front door. The stars were shining, ignoring the happenings down here. There was a glow off to the East. It wasn't the glow of city lights. It was the glow of fire. The night sky was pierced with the sounds of sirens in the distance. There were helicopters flying off to the North and JW recognized the distinctive percussive signature of detonations. He didn't know if it was munitions or storage tanks but he knew something had just exploded. It sounded like it had come from the river which was a little over five miles away from JW'S house. What they had heard was the sound of the Amtrak derailing as it rounded the bend before it crossed the river, but they didn't know it. They crossed the cul-de-sac. Evelyn was standing on her porch watching.

"Kate, I came outside and saw you and Josh a minute ago. I thought I heard gunshots." Evelyn said.

"You did." JW flatly. "Kate and Josh encountered some infected and they had to defend themselves. We are here to recommend you come over to our house tonight, we can help keep you safe." JW finished.

"Safe? From a virus? How do you propose to keep me safe from a virus? Do you have a cure?"

"Not from the virus Evelyn," Kate said. "From the infected. They attack. That is how it spreads."

"And how do you know that?" Evelyn questioned.

"I saw it." She said.

"Listen, I don't care if you come or not. But I am offering. If you want to stay in your home, stay. We will check on you in the morning." JW turned to walk away. Kate looked at him and started after. She looked back at Evelyn.

"Evelyn, please, if you change your mind. Come." Kate said.

Evelyn drew her jacket up a little tighter as she watched Kate follow JW back across the cul-de-sac. She wasn't sure what to do. If that crazy ass ex-army guy, who never ever speaks to her, came all the way over here to ask her to come stay with them for protection and his wife agreed with him, either they were a psycho-killer husband/wife duo or this might be an offer she needed to seriously consider.

JW and Kate had made it about halfway across the road when JW stopped. He turned and looked up the road to the buses. It was dark but he could make out the darker shapes lying on the ground where Kate and Josh had left them.

"I am sorry, you shouldn't have been out there." JW said.

"Bullshit. Whether I should have or shouldn't have doesn't matter anymore. Not tonight. What I have seen on the TV, on Scott's damn computers and with my own eyes is what matters. What I did was what needed to be done. I have been doing that our whole marriage. And now you need to realize something. That man, that man you keep inside, that man that scares you, that man that allowed you to do whatever you needed to do to come back home to me all those years ago, we need that man. I need you to make peace with it and be what we need you to be. For us."

"Ok." He started back to the house.

"Ok? Just like that?" she said.

"No, not just like that. But ok." He walked up the porch. "We have work to do."

When JW walked back inside Scott and Josh were sitting in the kitchen with a candle. He sat down with them.

"We have to secure this home. All interior doors have to come off so we can use them to cover the windows. We can push the Fridge in front of the kitchen door. We can push the couch against the front door and we can keep the garage door down. We only enter and exit through the front door if we have to go outside." JW rattled off his plan. "Let's get to work."

The next two hours were filled with hammers and nails. They managed to cover all the windows except the half-window over the sink. They used a couple of cookie sheets, screws, and JW's cordless drill to cover it. They were moving the refrigerator in front of the kitchen door when someone knocked on the front door. JW looked out the peephole.

"Come on in Evelyn." He opened the door and let her in. Kate met her and they walked into the living room.

JW and Josh pushed the couch up against the door. JW walked into the garage. The garage door had portholes, too small for anyone to get through but plenty big enough to watch the street. They faced Evelyn's house across the cul-de-sac and JW could see the cul-de-sac. What he couldn't see, because of the trees, was all the way back to the buses. He decided he would make patrols. He broke out the walkie-talkies from his hunting bag. He grabbed some fresh batteries and put them in. He walked into his room in the garage and opened his safe. He grabbed a box of pistol ammo and another magazine for the M4. He slung the rifle over his shoulder and left the safe open. He walked back into the kitchen.

"I can watch the street from the garage." He announced. "But I can't see the buses. I will go out every hour or so and just walk to where I can see up the road. I won't be out long. When I go I will take one of these." He showed them the walkie-talkies. "I want y'all all to rest as best you can. I will need someone to be awake each time I go out. Just in case."

He didn't need to say in case of what.

It was just past 11 when JW made his first walk outside. He woke Kate, who had managed to doze off sitting on the couch with Scott's head in her lap. Josh was asleep in his room and Evelyn was snoring loudly in JW and Kate's bed.

"Be careful." She said as he walked out the door.

She closed the door behind him and dead bolted the door. He walked out into the street and turned his flashlight off. The moon was bright and he could see a good ways up the road but not all the wall to the buses. He walked up the road until he could see them. He just stood there, listening. He could still hear sirens to the north and could still see the glow to his east. The sky was glowing in the direction of the sirens too. The helicopters were gone. He turned and walked back to the house. He made patrols all night long. He would just lie on the couch against the door between patrols. He looked at his watch. 4:30. He headed out again.

As he started up the road something caught his eye. Lights. Headlights. Pulling up to the bus. He crouched down and started moving towards them. The car stopped. He could see one person walk around from the driver's side and step in front of the car. He couldn't tell if there was anyone else. He crept closer. He could see there were two, maybe more. The first one had already climbed up on top of the hood of the bus and was reaching back. He pulled the one up and was reaching for the other one. When the first one jumped down onto the ground JW turned on his flashlight.

"Don't take another step." JW said.

"I told y'all we was on the right road." Bridger said, raising his hands and blinking in the light.

Reunion

JW stood there, seeing but not believing. He lowered the rifle. Bridger helped the other person down from the hood of the bus. JW had been so wrapped up in the things that were going on he had forgotten. He looked at Bridger and smiled. They had been through a lot together back during JW's old life. Bridger had covered his ass too many times to count and vice versa. And even though they had fallen out of close contact, and both of them knew why, none of that seemed to matter. He walked up and hugged Bridger.

"Good to see you brother." Bridger said.

"Good to see you too." He said.

"JW, this is Tilly and Raj. He's a doctor and she's a hoot," he laughed.

Tilly shot him a glance but amazingly held her tongue. Her and Raj lowered their hands.

"Is everything ok?" a voice came over the walkie.

"Yep, just fine. Bridger is here."

"Hey Katie" Bridger yelled over JW

"Hey Bridger" she replied.

"Honey, Bridger brought some friends. We've got company for breakfast, heading your way now." JW said.

They walked back to the house. Kate and Scott were up and as they came through the front door, Josh came stumbling out of his room. He stopped and watched as his Dad and Bridger and two strangers walked through the door.

"Hey Uncle Bridger." He called.

"Hey Josh, damn you grew up." He said walking towards him with his arms going out for a hug.

"Yep." Josh said, extending his hand for a handshake. Bridger took it and yanked him in for the hug, anyway.

They all went into the living room and sat down. Kate lit more candles and JW went to the kitchen. He turned on the stove. The gas was still on. He lit a burner and started pulling food out of the deep freezer. Kate had put as much as she could in the deep freezer when the power went out and it was still cold. He knew it wouldn't be for long. He started cooking sausage and bacon. He turned on another burner and started frying eggs. The living room grew quiet. The smell of food had made the group of travelers lose interest in recounting their story. Kate had heard enough to know what was happening on the other side of the buses. Chaos. They sat in the candlelight silently.

JW brought the plate of eggs and meat into the living room and had some paper plates tucked under his arm. Kate rose to help him and he asked her to grab the silver ware. They sat around the coffee table eating. He had boiled some water and found some instant coffee in the cabinet that he had forgotten about. He poured out cups. Tilly had finished eating and was lying on the couch. She was soon snoring. Raj lie down on the floor next to her and fell asleep. JW and Bridger leaned against the back wall.

"We need to bring my car inside your little compound." Bridger said. Smiling.

"Why?" JW asked.

"Because all my shit is in it and all their shit's in it." He said, nodding towards Tilly and Raj.

"Who are they?"

"Hell if I know, I came on them at a wreck. They were hurt. I helped them. Their car was crushed." He said.

"Yeah but why are they with you?" JW asked.

"Because I couldn't just leave them after what we saw."

"Why not?" JW asked.

"Because we're the good guys." Bridger smiled.

"Good answer." JW smiled too.

They had this conversation before. In a different time, in a different place, facing a decidedly different enemy. But they knew that it was a necessary conversation. They stood, JW nodded to Kate as they walked out the door. Kate nodded back. They walked outside up the road towards the buses.

"So what made you think to do this? With these?" Bridger said reaching out and touching the bus. The sun was beginning to come up. Everything had turned that gray color of early morning. Shapes took form.

"I just wanted to..." He broke off.

They became aware of someone walking on the road on the other side of the bus and knelt down to see. They could see bare feet and bare legs walking. JW stood up and opened the bus door. Bridger jumped up.

"JW, get your ass up here, you are not going to believe this."

JW climbed on the bus and looked out the window. In the street next to Bridger's car was an elderly woman. She was naked and wet. She had a shower cap on. She was just shuffling along. The bus driver's window was facing up the street so Bridger opened it.

"Hey" he called.

The woman stopped and without turning her body, turned her head towards Bridger's voice. Her shoulder turned and her arms swung with them. Then her legs finally started to pivot with her hips.

"Well shit, I guess I know why they call it

Marionette now. She looks like a fucking puppet on a string." Bridger observed.

JW turned his flashlight on the woman and they could see the opaque eyes and the slack skin. She screeched at the light and started towards it. JW handed the light to Bridger and shouldered his rifle. One shot. She fell. Bridger turned the light off.

"Well, I guess I don't really need to know where you stand on taking out these puppets." Bridger said.

"Puppet?" he asked

"Gotta call em something." Bridger said.

"Keep working on it." He continued, "I have seen enough to know they are dangerous and right now anything I think is dangerous to my family is dead. Period." He said.

"That's what I am counting on. Brother." Bridger smiled.

They started to get off the bus, JW turned to look back up the road. What had been an empty street one minute ago now had three or four people shuffling down it, in the direction of the bus.

"Damn." JW said.

Bridger looked back. He could see them too. He watched as another came out of the driveway just up the street. It turned towards the bus.

"You think they heard the shot?" Bridger asked.

"Maybe. Maybe they come to sound." He said.

They watched as the infected made their way down the street towards them. Each one made the same stuttered move as they walked. They would throw their upper body forward and their legs would shuffle under them. They repeated it over and over.

JW sat down in the driver's seat and Bridger was looking out the window behind him.

JW reached his hand out of the window and banged one time against the side of the bus. The reaction was instantaneous. They all jerked forward towards the sound. They weren't exactly running but continually falling forward with their legs moving just enough to keep them from falling down. They were a few yards from the bus and JW raised the rifle again. He dispatched each one until the street was empty again. They watched. Ten minutes passed and they didn't see anything else coming down the street.

"We need to get my stuff out of my car." Bridger said.

"I think I can spare a pair of clean socks if you need them." JW said.

"Thanks, I do, I didn't pack any. What I did pack was my bag of guns and I am pretty sure we are going to need those." He said.

JW cranked the bus and moved it so that Bridger could pull his car through. He parked the bus back, making sure there were no gaps someone could easily walk through. What he had seen in the last hour had made him realize that even though he could keep a vehicle from coming in, these things didn't drive. He would have to figure this out.

"What's it like out there?" JW asked nodding towards the buses.

"What do you mean?" Bridger asked.

"I haven't been a hundred yards outside those buses since we parked them." Yesterday he thought to himself. "My guess is that since these things are wandering the woods, things got worse since then."

"No shit, Sherlock. They have. I don't know what this is, but it is everywhere. If it's a virus, it's airborne. We encountered a family, isolated as hell, and one of them died of old age. He came back. No contact with anybody. Nothing. Just died and came back. I don't know if we are all just ticking time bombs or what but yeah, it got worse. Why?"

"I think we may have to go back out there." JW said, looking at the buses again.

On a String

This was a people problem. The more people, the more chance to become infected if this was a virus, and the more chance to encounter dead ones too. They needed to be away from people and not by just a few blocks and a bus. They needed to be miles away from folks. And JW had the perfect place. They just needed to figure out how to get there. They had figured out how to get out of a lot of tight spots. Some were bar fights in Fayetteville; others were gunfights not in Fayetteville. This was going to be basically the same thing. Just a simple forced march under fire. Except they weren't firing at you, they were trying to eat you. Bridger smiled.

"Basically the same." He mumbled.

"What?" JW said.

"Nothing" He smiled at JW.

JW looked at him turning his head sideways. He was glad Bridger was here. He was still having a hard time processing what happened with the deputy but he was beginning to put it in that place he keeps those things. That place was getting full and it took a little longer. Bridger had seen some of those things JW put away. That helped in a strange way.

"So you think this is the best move?" Bridger asked.

"Nope, but I have to go out there and see. Just a little recon job. I need to check out to the main road. I have to at least see that far. After that, well."

"Well?"

"Well nothing. One step at a time. Right now,

you say nothing. You just tell them I am doing a walk. Not anything else. Ok?" JW said.

"Yeah, I got that but why are you walking. Just use my car." Bridger said.

"No, I walk. I can see more. I need to be deliberate."

"Ok, your plan. I will be on the other end of that." pointing to the walkie in JW's pocket.

"You call if you need the cavalry."

"Will do, you just get back there and make sure everybody gets a present from your Santa bag." JW said.

"Ho, Ho, Ho" he smiled.

JW dropped to his belly and rolled under the bus. He had the rifle and his pistol. He stood and looked down the street. He had a little over a mile to the entrance where the four-way stop was. And probably a deputy's car. He glanced at the body just up the road. He started walking.

The sun was up over the trees now and he could see down the road. He didn't see any cars or people. As he reached the first house on the left, he glanced down at the deputy lying face down in the road. He reached down and rolled him over.

"I'm sorry". He said.

He reached into the deputy's pocket and grabbed his keys. He took the gun belt off him and put it on. Glock. Four mags. Flashlight, two pair of handcuffs and Taser. JW inventoried in his head. He started walking again. He moved slowly but deliberately. Had covered about half the distance to the main road without seeing anything. He had stopped a few times to listen to the sounds of helicopters off in the distance. None had approached.

"Hey, hey you." JW heard a voice to his right. He shouldered the rifle.

"Hey don't shoot." A man about JW's age was peaking out a side door of the house.

JW knew the house. He didn't know the man who lived here but Kate had told him the guy worked for the state too. He was a geologist or chemist or something.

"Please just don't shoot, I am not infected." He said.

"How do I know that?" JW asked

"Well, I am not trying to eat you."

"Fair enough" JW lowered the rifle.

"What are you doing out here?" He asked.

"I am walking to the main road to see what it looks like." JW said.

"It looks like a road. I know who you are. I saw you come rolling by yesterday in those buses. You're that," he hesitated "that guy that lives at the end of the road."

JW realized something. If you really want people to leave you alone, move into a neighborhood with a bunch of gossipy neighbors and don't take part in their gossip.

"I am just seeing what options are available. Choices." JW said. "How many folks are left?"

"I don't know about anything other than just these few houses right here." He waved his hand over about six houses up and down the street. He started pointing at each one.

"That one is gone. Dead. The next two are in the second house together, an elderly gentleman and a family of four. Except for the mom. She is in the other house. Dead but not dead. You know?" He raised his eyebrow at JW. JW nodded. "The rest on that side are dead or gone away. Some left this morning with the folks to my right. The couple to the left is inside my house with my daughter and her friend. We had a sleepover and we haven't been able to reach her parents. So 8, no 9, counting me."

"How do you know?"

"Know what?"

"About the house across the street, when was the last time you talked to them?"

"Well, it's been a few hours but there hasn't been any of those things out there."

"What news have you heard?" JW asked, less formally "I mean, besides the obvious."

"Well the only thing I have heard lately is on a battery powered police scanner. It was some police and some civilian talking. The lady was telling the cop that people were eating people and that blood was everywhere. There was no help. The cop was telling the lady to get to the shelter at the fairgrounds on the east side of town. She said she was at the fairgrounds."

"OK. Listen, I am going to walk to the main road. If you want me to, I can stop by on my way back. I am going to see if it's safe to leave." JW said.

"And go where?"

"Away from town. At least for a while." He said.

"Do you think it matters?"

"I don't know, but at least there will be less of those things."

"I don't know your name," he said.

"JW. JW Toles."

"Charlie. Charlie Fair." They shook hands.

"I'll stop by on my way back."

JW walked back out in the street. He walked on without encountering living or dead. He heard a few sirens and an occasional helicopter in the distance. Most of the cars were gone from driveways. A dog crossed the street in front of him. He could see the entrance to the neighborhood. He saw the deputy's car. He opened the trunk. There was a shotgun and another rifle in a built in case. There was also a big first aid kit and some road flares. He grabbed the shotgun and opened the driver's door. He mounted the shotgun in the rest and used the deputy's keys to crank the car. He turned out of the neighborhood slowly heading north towards the river and the bridge. He could see Kate's school ahead. It looked like folks had tried to gather there. Cars filled the parking lot. He thought about turning in but the windows in the building made him keep going. Every window was smeared in blood and handprints. Whatever had happened, it had been bad. He drove to the bridge and stopped. There was one car parked in the middle of the bridge with its door open. He knew he could get across the bridge. That was what he needed to know. He started to turn the car around and looked down the street towards town. He could see more vehicles. He had no reason to go towards town. He went anyway. He needed to know.

Charlie closed the door and his daughter looked at him.

"Who was that?" she asked.

"That was JW Toles. He lives at the end of the

road." He said.

"You mean that weird guy." She said, turning to her friend. "I heard he was like tortured and stuff when he was in the CIA and they messed with his brain."

"Jennifer, please. He is just a retired veteran who likes his privacy." He looked at her. She raised her eyebrows.

"OK he's a little weird." He said.

"Listen, he is talking about trying to get away from town. He says he has somewhere to go. I think we should consider going with him."

"Seriously?" she said.

"Seriously." Charlie said.

Bridger had told Kate that JW had gone to scout the neighborhood. He told her not told her not to worry. He told her a lot of things. It didn't matter. She had let him know in explicit detail what she thought of Bridger Preston allowing him to go out there. She had calmed down since but she still was worried. Raj and Tilly were sitting on the couch with Evelyn. Scott was sitting in JW's chair and Josh was sitting on the floor. Kate and Bridger came into the living room. Kate sat down on the floor.

"JW went out past the buses. He said he would be back soon. He was going to check out the rest of the neighborhood."

"By himself?" Raj asked.

"Yeah, he does that." Kate said.

"While we are waiting we need to figure out what we have and what we need. I have weapons for everyone. Anybody need a quick lesson just ask." Bridger said. "We also need to get all of our food together. We need to make sure it is ready to go." He paused. "Just in case." He added.

They all gathered around Bridger's bag. He had two pump shotguns with pistol grips, two

standard pump shotguns, three Colt AR Civilian
models and one honest to goodness Special Ops
issue M4 fully automatic rifle. That one was his.
It had been with him a long time. He also had
seven 9mm pistols of varying manufacturers. He
had some ammo but not much beyond what was
loaded in the weapons. He had several more
shotgun rounds and pistol rounds but most of
the other was what were in the magazines. Tilly
and Raj chose the standard shotguns. Josh and
Scott the pistol grips. They also had the rifles JW
had given them. Along with Kate's pistol, she
chose another pistol. Bridger took his M4 and
the magazines from the other rifles.

"Ok, everybody keep your friends close and your
guns closer." Bridger smirked.

They had brought some plastic totes in
already and began emptying the pantry.

"From now on, everything we have at all times,
has to be ready to go." Bridger added.

"I have food at my house too." Evelyn said.

"OK, we'll go get it. Raj, you wanna go with?" Bridger said.

"Ok." He looked at Tilly.

"I'm going too." Evelyn said. "It's my house, I need some things."

"Ok." Bridger said. He handed her one of the pistols.

"Do you know how to use it?"

"Point and shoot?" She said. He showed her the safety.

"Red is Ready. Then point and shoot."

They went to the front door. Bridger looked out the peephole. He didn't see any movement. They moved the couch away and opened the front door. The street was empty. He stepped out into the sunlight. They crowded out behind him onto the front porch. Being outside seemed foreign to them already. They had been hidden behind those boarded windows for less than a day and already the sun seemed new. Bridger, Raj and Evelyn started across the cul-de-sac. The others went back inside and closed the door. The group reached Evelyn's front door and slipped inside. She went into the kitchen and started pulling things out of her pantry. Raj started loading it into garbage bags that she had given him. Bridger went into the garage and found some totes to put stuff in. He also found a garden cart he could use to get it back across the street. He pulled the cart into the kitchen and started loading things up. They had just about emptied the pantry.

"I need to get some things out of my bedroom. Some personal things." She said.

"Ok. Need any help?" Raj said.

"No, no. Just some small things." She said as she went out of the kitchen.

Bridger and Raj finished packing everything onto the cart. They rolled the cart out the front door and went back inside to grab the other few bags. Bridger noticed the pictures on the wall. It showed a happy couple on vacation and at holidays. It showed pets, but no children. Raj came from the kitchen with the last bag.

"Where's Mrs. Collins?" he asked.

"Where's Mr. Collins?" Bridger asked, smiling.

"Dead" Evelyn said, walking from around the corner.

Bridger's smile went away. She walked past them and out the front door.

"Well, that was fun, let's go." Evelyn said.

Standing in her front yard between her and the cart were two of the infected. Her voice had carried when she opened the door and both turned to the sound. The closest one was wearing work coveralls with the CXT railroad emblem. The coveralls were shredded around the legs, ripped by the thick underbrush it had passed through. The hands looked the same except instead of cotton and nylon it was flesh and muscle that was torn apart. The tips of the fingers were bone, the flesh completely ripped away. Blood oozed through the coveralls. The same thorns had lacerated the face, the slack skin easily giving way under their sharpness. The other infected appeared to be a teenage girl. She was wearing shorts and a t-shirt. Her leg had been bitten. She had the same slack skin and pale eyes as the man. Both turned in that same jerky way Bridger had witnessed earlier. He raised the rifle. The first one jerked just as he fired and the round missed. It reached out and grabbed Evelyn. Raj fired over them as they fell and hit the other infected in the stomach. Bridger grabbed the one on Evelyn. Raj fired again. The girl (thing) in the yard fell. Bridger was holding on to the other with everything he had as it rapidly chomped for Evelyn's face. It was twisting and trying to turn and she was pushing it away as best she could. Raj tried to pull Evelyn from underneath it. They were all yelling. Boom. Everything exploded. Bridger fell backwards. The thing had quit struggling. Evelyn pulled herself from underneath with Raj's help. She had the pistol in her right hand. She was covered in what had come out of the back of the things head. They just stood there for a second, each looking at the other confirming they were all ok. Evelyn was crying, but just a tear or two. Bridger checked her over. Raj wiped her face off with a towel he grabbed from the kitchen.

"I'm fine. I'm fine. Just let me do that." She said, snatching the towel from him. "Sorry" she said.

"It's ok." He said.

They took a quick look around. They pulled the cart back across the cul-de-sac. The gunfire had alerted the others. They were standing in the front yard and rushed to the street to help when they saw them coming back. Tilly ran over to Raj and hugged him. Kate met Evelyn and helped her pull the cart. Bridger stopped and stood in the middle of the cul-de-sac. He looked up the road towards the buses. He looked at his watch. Not time to worry yet.

He had another hour before he was even overdue. He looked at the sun, climbing higher in the sky. Nice weather, he thought. He turned and followed Raj and Tilly.

JW had reached the Home Depot. It was on the edge of the main part of town. Past the Home Depot was the college and just south of the college was downtown. He had encountered several infected but only randomly and he drove by them. As he approached the store, he could see more in the parking lot, wandering around. He stopped the car and opened the glove box. Binoculars. He scanned the road ahead of the store and could see several more in the street. He walked to the back fence of the store and found a gate. He approached the back of the store and climbed the ladder mounted for the AC service. He got on the roof and walked to the front of the store. When he got to where he could see, he paused. The parking lot didn't just have some infected. It was full of them. He could see loudspeakers mounted on poles. There was some kind of aid station set up in the adjacent field the store had used for outbuilding displays. There were dozens more infected shuffling in and out of the shelter. He had seen enough. He climbed back down. He convinced himself that what he wanted to do was the right move. He knew that it was a lie. It wasn't the right move. It was the only move. And it probably wasn't enough. He drove towards home.

Charlie Fair and his daughter walked back to their house. The group across the street were staying put. The couple that had taken shelter with Charlie, Amanda and Chris Bettis, were going to stay with Charlie. If he left they left. Counting them, his daughter and her friend Lori, Charlie's group totaled five. He told his daughter to start packing whatever food they have; he was going to make sure they were ready to go, if the time came.

"So do we need to pack clothes?" Amanda asked.

"Yep. I'll help." Charlie said. He and the couple headed next door.

"I don't want to leave. My parents, my brother. I don't know what happened to them. I can't leave." Lori said after they left.

"Lori, we have too." Jennifer said.

"Why?"

"Because we have too." They kept packing.

Charlie was in the neighbor's kitchen loading the food into plastic Magix bags. Chris brought in a few smiley face boxes to load the bags into. Amanda brought two suitcases from the bedroom and proclaimed that they were ready. Charlie put the bag into the box and they headed back next door. They could see someone walking down the road. They watched as it shuffled along. It turned towards the sound of a

dog barking. They hurried inside. Charlie looked back as the police car pulled up.
"Be ready. Sometime this afternoon." JW said out the driver's window of the police car.

"How will we know it's time to go?" Charlie asked.

"It'll be just like being a kid again." JW drove off. Charlie walked inside shaking his head.

"Weird guy" he thought.

JW drove past the one infected walking the street. He parked the police car all the way past the buses. He crawled under and walked towards his house. He saw the two bodies lying in Evelyn's yard. He walked to his front door and knocked. He could hear them moving the couch and the dead bolt being opened. Scott opened the door. They hugged. He walked inside. Kate heard him come in and they all walked into the living room. Evelyn and Raj were sitting on the couch and Tilly came out of the bathroom and sat between them. Bridger was standing in the kitchen doorway. Josh was on the floor.

"I went to town. I got as far as the Home Depot. It all appears overrun," he continued, "The aid shelter was full of them. I don't think there is anything left. Anyone down there is either one of them or going to be if they don't get out. And that is what we are going to do."

"What?" Evelyn asked.

"We are going to get out. We are going to leave." He said.

"And go where." Raj asked.

"Nowhere, well actually the middle of nowhere." Bridger said.

"What the hell are you talking about?" Tilly said.

"I have a piece of land and right now I think being as far away as possible from populated areas is the best way forward. We can load up everything we have in the buses."

"Oh great, the Partridge fucking family goes

camping." Tilly said. JW cut her a glance.

"I'm Keith." Bridger said. Earning a glance of his own.

"We need to get everything packed up. All the food, anything we think we need." He said. "Anybody have anything questions?"

"For how long?" Evelyn asked.

"I don't know." He said. "We need to carry everything we can. We will take the two buses and Kate's SUV. My truck is already up there."

"Why?" Bridger asked.

"Why is my truck there? Long story." JW said, absentmindedly rubbing his head. "Why the buses? So we can carry more stuff but more importantly, when we get there, we can use them for shelter. We need to leave as soon as we can. I found another family in the neighborhood. We will stop to pick them up. After that we don't stop. I scouted all the way to the bridge. It is clear. Once we get across the bridge, I will stay ahead of the buses in the SUV. Kate you drive the first bus, Bridger you follow. Get everything ready. We move the buses in one hour. Let's get to work." He said. They started packing.

Caravan

JW and Kate stood in their bedroom. It was really the first time they had been completely alone together since this all started. She sat on the bed as he changed clothes.

"How you doing?" She asked.

"Huh?"

"How are you doing? Are you okay?" she asked again.

"I'm trying. Right now I am focused on getting us away from this."

"Ok. You don't have to do all the heavy lifting.

We have a plan. We know what to do."

He finished getting dressed and they walked back into the living room. They had managed to fill it with boxes and totes of food, blankets, clothes and anything else they thought they needed. Everyone sat on a box or on the couch.

"Ok. Here's the plan. Bridger, Kate and I will go get the buses. The rest of you start moving everything into the garage. When we get back, we'll pull one bus against the garage and the other in the street. We'll load everything and everybody in one bus. The other bus will be just Bridger and Raj, it is Raj right?" JW said. Raj nodded. "I'll lead, Kate you next with everybody on board, then Bridger. Everybody be on alert. We don't know when these things are going to show up.

"Everybody ready?" They nodded.

JW, Kate and Bridger walked out the front door and up the road to the buses. The sun had given way to clouds and it looked like the day was going to end in rain. They opened the door to the first bus as the drops began to fall. Bridger climbed on board followed by JW. They looked up the street. A few infected wandering at the far end of what they could see. Nothing else. They cranked up the bus and Bridger climbed off. Kate had the other bus running.

"Y'all pull down. Get everything loaded. I will watch the road. Now go." Bridger said.

JW and Kate pulled their buses down the cul-de-sac. Kate parked by the garage and JW parked in the street. He climbed down and went to where they were loading up. He grabbed his backpack out of Josh's car. He grabbed his toolbox, the first-aid kit from the deputy's car, an axe and a couple of other tools and threw them on the bus. He loaded the weapons still in his gun safe into the SUV. He walked back down the driveway and waved up the street to Bridger. He made sure everybody was loaded into the bus. He jumped in Kate's SUV and started to pull away, he looked back to make sure everyone was in line behind him. They set off.

Charlie was looking out his front door peephole. A bus pulled up to his driveway and opened the door.

"Just like being a kid again." He smiled. "Let's go everybody. They're here."

JW parked and got out of his car. He was watching the street. Bridger stood in the stairwell of his bus. The first infected came from between the houses, by the time Bridger saw it there were at least a dozen more coming from behind the houses. Tilly and Raj were helping get the last few things from the house. Amanda was coming out of the door with them. The rest were halfway to the buses. JW ran towards the group trying to carry suitcases down the driveway.

"Go, go get to the bus. NOW!!" he said in a muffled shout.

They paused, surprised. The first screams

caused the infected to react. Bridger jumped down from his bus and covered one side of the driveway while JW was holding the other. Shots rang out of the bus windows from Josh, Kate and Scott. Most of the infected fell away. Charlie's group dropped everything and ran for the bus. Tilly and Amanda were coming out of the house when one of the infected came around the other side of the house. It was a girl, no more than 7 or 8 years old. It grabbed Amanda by the arm, Amanda jerked away from the small hands. She screamed. Tilly leveled the shotgun at its head and fired. It exploded. The child's body fell, headless to the ground. Amanda screamed again.

"Oh the humanity and all that shit, I get it. Now shut the fuck up before you get us killed." Tilly said.

One of the infected that JW shot fell at the feet of Charlie's daughter, she stopped and screamed. Everyone behind rushed against her and the whole group went down. Most of the infected were down too.

"Ok folks, everybody up and on the bus." JW said reaching out to help them up.

The gunfire from the bus had stopped. Bridger was dispatching the few infected still coming from behind the house. Tilly, Raj and Amanda made their way down the driveway.

"Come on folks, don't have all fucking day." Tilly said. "It's just the fucking zombie apocalypse." Earning a few disapproving looks from the newcomers.

Tilly grabbed the suitcases, strolling around the bodies. She loaded them one at a time onto the back of the bus.

"Wouldn't want you to lose your panties." She said, climbing back on the bus. JW and Bridger gave each other an approving smile. JW didn't know where Bridger found this girl, but she had her moments.

They stood outside the bus. JW, Kate and Bridger. The rest were hanging their heads out listening. It was time.

"OK here we go. From this point on we do not plan on stopping." JW said. He hugged Kate. He looked up in the bus at his two sons.

"Saddle up." He and Bridger shook hands.

They slowly pulled to the end of the neighborhood. They turned left. As they passed a few houses, they saw odd sights. Signs haphazardly painted on the doors. Help us, mainly. They occasionally saw a curtain move or a shadow pass by the window. No way to tell if it was living or dead. As they passed a church, its door flung open. The sound of the passing buses had awoken the congregation. They were streaming out in the same falling, stumble run they had seen before. Jennifer and Lori were looking out of the back of the bus. They could see the other bus behind them and the crowd of infected beyond that. They drove on. Kate was not prepared for the sight of her school. Cars abandoned, some burnt. Tents torn down and scattered. She could see the same windows JW had seen earlier. She knew which one was her classroom. She could see it as she passed the building. Tears came down her face as she saw the streaks of blood. They drove on. They approached the bridge.

JW stopped. What had been an empty bridge two hours ago now had a small gang of infected wandering around the car he had seen earlier. He stepped out of the SUV and walked back to Kate's bus.

"Tell Josh to come up here and drive my car." He said.

Josh came out of the bus. JW saw Bridger walking up to him.

"Raj can drive my bus, I'll help." He said.

They walked around the SUV and started towards the bridge with the buses following behind. Bridger and JW methodically cleared the path. There were infected wearing military uniforms. Bridger took the opportunity to relieve them of any weapons as they passed by. From the variety of clothing among the others it appeared these were the poor souls who had encamped at the school. JW could see children and women among the infected. As they moved the caravan followed. They made their way around the car on the bridge. Once they made it across the bridge they stopped. JW climbed back in the SUV with Josh and Bridger back to his bus. They set out once again.

Tilly sat in the back of the bus. She rolled down the road looking at the smoke filled pine trees as the rain brought the smoke down to the ground. The fading light still provided enough for her to be able to make out the burnt out structure of the night before as they passed. She didn't know where they were, but she knew where she was.

"About twenty more miles." Scott said over the back of the seat in front of her.

"What?" she said.

"Twenty more miles until we get there. I come up here all the time. I think it is going to be a good place."

"A good place for what?" she asked.

"I don't know, a good place to get our heads together and figure out what to do next."

"And what is next?" she asked. He didn't answer.

Bridger was sitting in the first seat of the bus he and Raj were using. They both saw the dirt road and smoke. They didn't talk about it. "What the hell?" Raj said, looking in his rearview mirror.

Bridger stood and walked down the aisle to the back of the bus. He looked out the window and saw two cars following them. He grabbed the walkie.

"JW, we have picked up a convoy. Two vehicles,

unknown occupants."

"Ok, I am going to stop. If they stop behind you, wait for me to walk back."

"Aye aye cap'n" Bridger said.

As they slowed to a stop and pulled to the side of the road, the vehicles stopped too. Bridger watched them. Nobody got out. JW walked to the last bus and Bridger came out. They walked to the first car. JW approached the driver's window. It was down. A woman and two kids.
"Why are you following us?" he asked.

"We were at the school. We hid in our cars and didn't move. We haven't seen anyone come by in hours. You were the first ones we saw, we couldn't stay there any longer."

"The people behind you?" he asked.

"Neighbors. I'm Janice Walker. My son, Jeremiah and my nephew Clyde. Behind us are the Harrison's. An older couple who lived next door." She said.

"We are going to the woods. We have some provisions and we have weapons. If you would like to follow us, you are more than welcome. But, if you do, you follow our rules."

"OK. What are your rules?" she asked.

"Simple. Stay alive so you can keep others alive." He said.

She nodded her head. He walked to the other vehicle and had the same conversation. They would follow. He told them to get behind Kate's bus and let Bridger follow. They were growing their caravan.

Ahead JW could see the turn. They had seen a few vehicles abandoned on the way here, but not many. The road was fairly clear once they had crossed the bridge. A few houses and a few stores. They had seen no people. Living or dead. That was good. JW turned down the dirt road. Once he got everyone through the gate, he locked it. They made camp. JW got his truck started and they built a small fire. Tilly and Evelyn had taken upon themselves to coordinate sleeping arrangements. No one wanted to sleep. The darkness of the night was accentuated by the ghostly whispers of smoke lit by the moon. Charlie had brought a weather radio and was cranking it.

"Forecast for the weekend. Zombies. More at five." Tilly said, watching him crank.

He turned on the power. Static. He moved the dial. Static. He switched bands. Static. He switched to AM and all the way to the left of the dial, he got a signal.

■ ı

PLEASE STAND BY FOR A MESSAGE FROM THE VICE PRESIDENT OF THE UNITED STATES.

PLEASE STAND BY FOR A MESSAGE FROM
THE VICE PRESIDENT OF THE UNITED
STATES.
■■■

The message repeated several times.
Charlie was just about to turn the dial and try
another station.

■■■

"This is Vice President Addison. Tonight
we mourn the loss of so many, including
President Wilson. I come to you tonight as a
father and a friend. Washington has fallen. All
information we have is that the city has been
completely over run with Marionette. We have
lost contact with all overseas military
commands. We are at a secure location in
Colorado and although we have contained it for
now, it is inside the compound. People listening
to my voice; please hold those you love tight

tonight when you say your prayers. Stay strong. Be safe. God bless.

■■■■■■■■■■■■■■■■■■■■■■■■■■■■■■■■■■■■■■■ ⁞

The group around the campfire looked at each other. All were searching the faces of strangers to find hope.

"We made it here. We are still here." Raj said.

Everyone slowly went to their bus. Nobody was sleeping. Everyone was sitting in a seat. Looking out the window into the darkness. Kate, Scott and Josh were sitting at the front of one bus. With them were people who joined the caravan past the bridge, and Evelyn Collins. The other bus held Tilly, Raj and Charlie's group, Jennifer, Lori, Amanda and Chris. Both buses passed the night watching the moon dance off the wet left by the rain and the smoke drifting through the trees.

"You were at the school?" Kate asked Janice.

"Yes."

"What happened?"

"It...it was bad. We were...just..."

"It's ok, we can talk tomorrow. Just rest." Kate said.

When the sun finally rose JW and Bridger walked down the road towards the gate. They cut through the woods. The came to the end of the stand of trees they were in and it opened into a field. They could see the road from this spot. Even though JW knew it wasn't on his land, he didn't think things like that were going to matter as much any more. The started across the field just to see what they could see.

"It looks like your plan might work." Bridger said.

"For now. But for how long, this thing has spread so fast. There wasn't even enough time to think. All we did was react."

"Lucky we had a chance to." Bridger said.

"From everything we have seen we were very lucky. But yeah, for right now, we are ok."

"We might have another problem."

"What's that?" JW asked.

"We have maybe three weeks of food. Tops." He said.

"You remember laughing me off the phone about zombies in Madagascar?"

"Yeah." Bridger smiled and looked down.

"That was four days ago. Four days. Three weeks seems like a long time." He said, looking at the sunrise. "Besides, we've got the rest of our lives to figure it out."

Music for Marionette

Lincoln Durham

The Wailin' Jennys

Willie Nelson

Bob Dylan

Shovels and Rope

The Be Good Tanyas

The Kills

The Dirty River Boys

The White Stripes

David Allen Coe

The next book in the Marionette series

Walk with Me

by

S.B. Poe

Coming June 1, 2018

Marionette

Printed in Great Britain
by Amazon

25916193R00108